¡AZÚCAR!
A NOVEL

ALSO BY NII AYIKWEI PARKES

Poetry
eyes of a boy, lips of a man
M is for Madrigal
Ballast
The Makings of You
The Geez

Fiction
Tail of the Blue Bird

For Children
Tales from Africa

As Editor
Tell Tales: Volume 3
Dance the Guns to Silence: 100 Poems for Ken Saro-Wiwa
X-24 unclassified: a ccollection of short stories
South of South
Filigree

¡AZÚCAR!
A NOVEL

NII AYIKWEI PARKES

PEEPAL TREE

First published in Great Britain in 2023
Peepal Tree Press Ltd
17 King's Avenue
Leeds LS6 1QS
UK

ISBN 13: 9781845235475

Printed in the United Kingdom
by Severn, Gloucester,
on responsibly sourced paper

MIX
Paper from
responsible sources
FSC
www.fsc.org
FSC® C022174

Supported using public funding by
ARTS COUNCIL
ENGLAND

For Naa Naa, Fifi and Afi

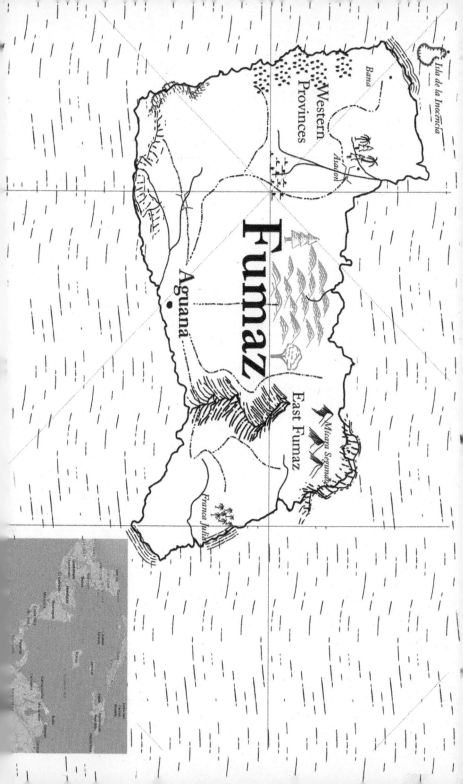

Soñada Family

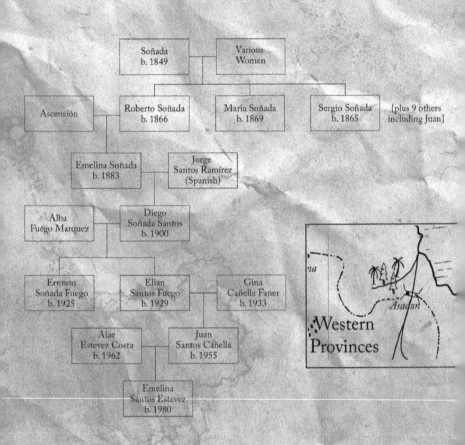

Soñada
b. 1849

Various
Women

Ascensión

Roberto Soñada
b. 1866

María Soñada
b. 1869

Sergio Soñada
b. 1865

(plus 9 others
including Juan)

Emelina Soñada
b. 1883

Jorge
Santos Ramírez
(Spanish)

Alba
Fuego Marquez

Diego
Soñada Santos
b. 1900

Ernesto
Soñada Fuego
b. 1925

Elian
Santos Fuego
b. 1929

Gina
Cañella Faner
b. 1933

Alae
Estevez Costa
b. 1962

Juan
Santos Cañella
b. 1955

Emelina
Santos Estevez
b. 1980

Western
Provinces

Asadon

Let us begin with a single note of music, speaking neither of tone nor tempo, for this is where it began. We can know nothing except for the pose of Emelina Santos in that moment, which, in the light that reflects off the shifting face of the waters by the Malecón, spoke of liberty and entrapment. For when we speak of losing ourselves in music, in the same flight and flurry of muscle contractions that make us feel so liberated, are we not also chained to the enchantment of the song's sway, slaves to its syncopation? But let us not debate this contradiction for too long. Rather, let's hold this moment, this image of a woman arrested like a music note that triggers a memory deep enough to get lost in. And this image, in silhouette, sits in the irises of a man the texture of night, sits so long it leaves its imprint, becomes his pupils.

★

In 1959, the year Fumaz, our great, green, island country, freed itself from the tyranny of churches and colonial impositionists, no one would have believed you if you said that our president would become a victim of his own decree that the *person* – for he was nothing if not a man who believed in equality for all, and we all know women can grow beards too… that the person with the longest beard would be the ruler of the land. But to see him now, bent double with the weight of a wiry waterfall that he hired more and more people to help him clean, you couldn't help but feel that he, Guerrero Candia Rosario Austral – Guerrero Rosario for short – had enslaved himself. Guerrero was a peopleist who had aligned our land with the Union of Soviet Socialist Republicans, much to the annoyance of the United States of the Americas, who felt their half-century colonial subjects should at least show some loyalty to those who first exploited their land and labour. I pause here to point out that for the people of Fumaz, the Fumazero, there was great entertainment found in arguing about the aforementioned states (USSRs and USAs) as they sounded the same when abbreviated – something along the lines of USERs. The previous dictator, nicknamed Papá Güey, had the unrestrained approval of USAs since he kept his excesses limited to flaying the flesh of his own people, not flirting with other users.

In any case, I only mention Guerrero Rosario because his actions had a direct impact on the genesis of the history I am to recount. His choice of fraternal nation led to the USAs enacting an embargo on imports from Fumaz in 1962, which meant that there was plenty of sugar with no buyer. For a few days after the announcement reached our island, it was not uncommon to see young Fumazero farm folk, gleaming with a sheen of sweat and sugar, dancing in protest along the same country roads they had jubilated on with drum, song and dance following Guerrero Rosario's ascent to power. Pursued by flies, and assaulted by ants when they stood still, they created an almighty buzz that lingered in the air long after they had passed. The fuss was soon calmed when the USSRs stepped in to buy the surplus sugar to annoy their eternal rivals in trade, arms and exploitation. It was then the idea first took root in the head of Diego Soñada Santos – already in his distinguished years – of watering his rice paddies with sugar solution so that his rice would be sweeter than any of his competitors' harvest.

Now, had the paler Santos side of Diego's heritage not been

10

so successful at suppressing the history of the duskier Soñada side, he would have known that his idea of marrying sugar and rice was hardly original. Of course, the Santoses were only being savvy, for in a land where a majority of the people were the colour of a water-soaked log, yet an unpigmented canine with a name like Benito was treated better than any curly-haired girl called Amina, it had been wise to be a selective storyteller.

The truth is, in the middle of the 19th century, the original Soñada – self-named, as the moniker his enslaved mother whispered to him at birth would do little to help him in a land that only offered humanity to that which had a Spanish name – raised legendary pigs on a diet of sugar-coated remnants of rice-husking.

Born free before Segismundo Moret and his colleagues managed to negotiate freedom for all wombs, due to a deal struck by his parents with their master Hector Ruiz, Soñada founded his empire with a sickly sow that turned out to be pregnant and soon had an unruly farrow that the boy could barely contain in his quarters. Unwilling to sell them before they had grown, he walked them like dogs, feeding them his special rice-sugar mix by hand and letting them graze without permission in spaces that were not open to boys like him.

As soon as they were old enough, it became clear that he had a star in his spotted boar, Luchando – a perfectly proportioned pig that gave rise to speculation that his sire was a wild hog – the kind that practised mating as a competitor sport. A new line of business opened for Soñada; he hired Luchando out to owners of sows for a flat fee, or a share of the offspring. By the time Luchando had himself become sugar-cured ham, Soñada was a wealthy man at just fifteen years of age. He owned two horses and a cart marked *Luchando – a real dog of a pig*.

Soñada himself was not one for retreating when it came to being forward with a woman. With his athletic build, deep dimples and his trademark clean, tan sack coat that concealed his dagger, paired with pristine white linen trousers and black boots, he stood out from general workers, more formally-dressed landowners and the men of the Spanish navy in uniform. Delivering ham on his cart, he left many a European esposa with extra rations of meat.

With their men increasingly called away to quell uprisings – on and off Fumaz – inspired by the exploits of Eutimio Mambí in Santo Domingo, the lives of the few European women still on the island had turned lonely. To have an energetic, evidently cultured, young man to whom they could teach the finer arts of lovemaking, who listened to instructions and laughed as though a volcano had erupted in his chest, was a blessing they could scarce refuse.

Like his late boar, Luchando, Soñada took to mating with an eagerness that led to whispers at balls, and orders for ham coming by messenger from all over the island – far beyond the Western Provinces, where he lived, even as far as the capital, Aguana.

On the occasions when their indiscretions came to life, kicking in their wombs like an internal rebellion before emerging tight-haired, fists balled and smiling, the esposas employed the knowledge of their husbands' drunken excursions to the servant quarters to their advantage. When asked about the appearance of a mulatto child in the house, the wives would respond: "One of the girls got pregnant so I sent her away after the birth. Should I call her back so we can find out what happened?"

"No need." A sheepish grin would flash. "You did the right thing; these natives are wild."

This is how Soñada's children were conveniently cared for by servants under the eyes of guilt-ridden husbands who secretly taught their bastard children the alphabet. When Soñada arrived on later visits to find his progeny flourishing among the barely-heeded throng of toddlers weaving between the boots and skirts of the household's harried staff, he took them with him in his cart to his growing household, where his parents cared for them.

All told, Soñada had twelve children, seven – all male – born before he was married in 1873, and five girls, born on the farm he had pieced together from small adjacent plots bought from Spanish landholders struggling to hold off the invasion of investors from the USAs. The daughters you will hear about later, for they were born in a time when a woman hid her true powers, or maybe you won't hear about them, but you will know their power, you will know the world they made. The winds of our island will tell you that one who tells a story is but a reflection of what was overheard and what was seen, but not much else. Repeating what was overheard makes parrots of storytellers, not crows; they have the words, but not the wisdom. Even their voices change, for it is not their own words they speak. It is for the listener to match what is said with what can be seen.

In any case, starting with a handsome sum given to them by their father, all the sons became traders, supplying goods and arms to the many parties seeking to profit from Fumaz. The son of interest to us is Roberto Soñada, who relocated to Aguana to trade at the harbour – the West Harbour.

To understand Roberto's business practice, you have to understand what the harbours were like. It was wild in those days, everything was swept aside for profit – scruples, dead rats, friendships, even national duty. Imagine two harbours, less than a mile from each other because they are, in fact, the fingers on the hand of a person who lost three fingers to a sharp blade in a quarrel with a bloodthirsty rival – you are looking from the direction of the sea, with the fingers as the sea. The harbours share an entry to the sea – the wrist of this crippled hand – and are split two ways – as if the cruel tyrant who cut the fingers spread them apart as far as they would go before snipping off the selected three.

The East Harbour was run by pirates and vagabonds; everyone knew that. You only went there to do business if you had crooked intentions or merchandise.

This is not to say that the West Harbour was much better; it was crammed with its own brand of hustlers, more subtle, but no less ruinous if you fell for their patter. Beneath the shadows cast by the sails of wooden ships, along uneven passages with stone and mud underfoot, food tables stood side-by-side – closer to the quays than they were allowed to be, and hastily moved backwards whenever a West Harbour official's approach was announced by a network of barefoot boys dotted along the bank. Behind them, dark wooden buildings for incoming and outbound goods, separated by a wide expanse filled with carts and muscled porters, stretched back towards the city.

On the long tables were a bounty of enormous pots of black beans around which clouds of flies buzzed; pyramids of oranges; boiled tamales (left in water to keep moist); roasted corn on the cob; fecund-smelling guavas (with the odd one sliced to reveal its rude pink insides); grilled plantains; wilting salads (that were ignored by all but the procurement crew of steam-powered, metal battleships); stews in a range of colours; and the stranger-looking fruits our island offers, such as soursop and the dragon fruit the Chinese came with. Between the tables were gaps that could swallow you whole. Out of one you might hear some irresistible music, even see a well-heeled man grasping the double bass that keeps the music steady.

But step a little closer and a woman would place a hand on your thigh. "So you like to move, eh? I can keep you moving all afternoon," she'd say, the rest of her sculpted body appearing from the shadows to lean on your shoulder as the bassman winks his endorsement in your direction.

You'd be half-awed, half-enchanted. You'd wonder if the bassman was a pimp, but he is more than that. The moment you followed the sashaying woman to the shack where she made men scream, you were caught in a house of commerce that would insist on supplying your every need. They would convince you to buy your sacks of rice, your ham, sugar, cheese, flour, cloth, drinking water, salt – everything from them. Then they would go to the real suppliers and negotiate a discount that ensured them a handsome profit and then add to the real price to further ensure the handsomeness of that profit.

That is what the harbours were like. Middlemen could cut your profit to barely liveable shreds – and that is why Roberto was constantly on edge, offering newer, crazier enticements to the shifting hordes of men the ships spat out.

His marriage of rice and sugar came by accident. A range of snacks made by his sister Maria often sat in his store. Roberto liked to joke that she made almost as much profit as he did without leaving their homestead, yet he happily displayed on his counter the cakes and tarts and sweets she made, because they were bright lures. One week, a bag of sugar sweets she had made sat on his counter and every day sailors buying rice and ham from him took a handful. Almost a year later, two of them came back and asked for these sweets again, as they believed they had helped stop their gums from bleeding. Unable to spare the time to duplicate Maria's recipe – which was simply a combination of water, sugar and lime juice, boiled and rolled into rough shapes – he mixed sacks of sugar with lime juice and gave small bags of this lime sugar to anyone who bought more than two sacks of rice from his store. Before long, the word had spread, much like the diseases that plagued the harbours, and Roberto was the most successful rice merchant in the West Harbour.

His wooden store remained, its attendant trees rooted,

restless and raspy as ever, but he built a stone building close to the harbour, with living quarters upstairs and a high-ceilinged grain store downstairs. On a slight incline by the track that led back to his father's homestead in the Western Provinces, the building reflected Roberto's life in business – a solid foundation, with touches of serendipity in the later stages of its evolution. The courtyard behind the building was an afterthought, but the land became available and it was handy for planting vegetables and having a compact stable for his horses. The living quarters were then adjusted to sit above the stable and enclose the courtyard, creating an open rectangle of six rooms facing the original residence, connected by a balcony and two oddly-shaped doors chiselled out of stone walls – one on the right leading into the kitchen, the other connecting to Roberto's bedroom on the left. The house became a stopping place for Roberto's siblings and their families. In time, many of his nephews and nieces would stay while studying at universities in Aguana, their youthful exuberance imbuing the house with a perpetual air of celebration. Many stone buildings were built next to it and they would become the foundation of what we now know as L'Aguana Vieja, where many of the old stores have now become hotels or clubs. Roberto's building was never sold; it went through many transitions, and during Guerrero Rosario's revolution it housed meetings for young revolutionaries, dance and exercise sessions for older Aguanans, but it never left the family.

So, when Emelina Santos visited Fumaz in 1999 for her great-grandfather, Diego Soñada Santos' 99th birthday – as the old man had declared 99 a more momentous occasion than 100 – it was where she stayed, and when looking for a place to experience the night life of Aguana, she only had to go five houses away to be embraced by samba, salsa, live horns. It was music as she had never heard it in USAs, where she was born and raised, and it triggered something in her; she knew she would return. On stage that night, watching her abandonment of self to music, was a man who had come to the Isla de la Inocencia on a scholarship in 1983, escaping drought in his own country to become an agriculturist. Having left Ghana at thirteen, Yunior became a man in Fumaz, during a troubled period that Guerrero Rosario called *half-time*, starting in 1991, during which house pets became family meals for lack of meat. Even Aguana Zoo reported losses; turtles, an ostrich, buffalo, okapi and two talking parrots gone forever silent.

His name was not Yunior; it was Oswald Kole Osabutey Jnr. When the Spanish tutor first asked for his name, he had said it clearly, but Profesor Hernandez had forgotten, and the next time he called Oswald to conjugate a verb, instead of pointing and asking what his name was, as he did with some of the other students – mainly boys from Angola, Southern Sudan, Cape Verde and a sprinkling of girls – Profesor Hernandez snapped his fingers and blurted out, "Yunior."

Overwhelmed by the newness of everything – the fertile green of our vegetation he could see clearly from his seat by the open window, the weight of concentration it took to follow what he was being taught, the thickness of our Cs and dip of our double Ls, Oswald Kole Osabutey Jnr. opted for the safest utterance – "Si," he responded.

He was never called Oswald after that.

When they played football in the open yard between the teaching and boarding buildings in his compound, shouts of *Yunior* rang out whenever he had to pass the ball or dribbled past two, three, four opposing players, or scored one of the spectacular goals he became known for, with his team mates piling on top of him in celebration, cementing the name in myth and reality.

Yunior's Escuela Secondaria was one in a cluster of five lettered A to E. They were enclosed by a perimeter of barbed wire, anchored at intervals to pillars of solid concrete. When Yunior first arrived, he felt as though he had been sent to a prison. The carefully trimmed bushes lining the enclosure, for all their occasional flourish of rogue papaya or mango trees bursting oranges, yellows and reds like lanterns in the uniform green, did not conceal the kinked metal threads. It looked like the military barracks he had passed by in trotros near Cantonments in Accra. It wasn't what his mother had described, what his father read out: *A safe, secluded environment where your child will learn Spanish and all the required secondary level subjects before progressing to sponsored higher education of a world class standard.*

Yunior had jumped at the chance. He didn't like the secondary school he had started in Accra; Christian Methodist Secondary School's uniform consisted of brown shorts and a deep purple shirt, which he detested. At twelve, he had been the youngest in his first year of secondary school and was picked on continually. It didn't help that he was small for his age and unconsciously broke into song sometimes, drawing more attention to himself. Some of his classmates were starting secondary school at fifteen or sixteen, after hard lives selling groundnuts, coconuts, air fresheners, puppies, newspapers and sweets as hawkers on Accra's roads to pay meagre contributions towards their education. They were already world weary before they started to learn about the world from books.

Yunior had never had to sell anything. His mother, Naa Okailey, was a food trader who worked at the central market close to their home in Adabraka, earning more money than his father, a minimally-skilled government clerk. She had invested faithfully in Yunior's education, but with two younger kids, she was relieved when her husband came home with the application form for the Fumazero scholarship. It wasn't that she thought they couldn't continue to scrape enough together for Yunior's education, but working under an increasingly hot sun in the market, she had seen the ground turn harder, bereft of rain; she'd heard the prices of food, shouted across zigzagging walkways, shoot higher; she'd smelled the despair in the air as even she, for all the friends she had who were bakers, had to send Yunior to queue for bread.

Ghana had fallen under the spell of dry Sahel winds and the ensuing drought was biting hard. Fewer people were buying the cooking oil Naa Okailey sold in smaller, repackaged units at the market. Some of her friends who sold vegetables had stopped coming to the market altogether as they could not reliably make up the daily fee they paid for their stalls – crammed squat-spaces where the traders sat on stools and arranged their bright produce in artful heaps on wide wood trays. The gaps they left, previously as sought after as gold dust, were now covered in common dust. For rice, one had to go to one of the Food Distribution Corporation outlets around the city with a chit. When local corn ran out and some aid finally came from the West, there were queues for yellow corn, a variety so alien that it drove old ladies half-mad – corn was supposed to be white. All things were rationed. The lines of chit-bearing families grew longer and more dust-beaten as the year progressed.

And then the Agege-Ghanaians – omo Ghana – started to arrive with their sad tales, new dances, and memories of Chief Commander Ebeneezer Obey's wedding song and King Sunny Ade's velvety voice – Fuji music. Thousands and thousands of them, more numerous than the wilting trees that mourned along their route: warring clusters of acacia, neem and guava in Agbara and the gap-toothed French order of palms on the roads of Benin, broken further by the bridge over Lagune de Cotonou where the smell of the sea at Grand Popo and Lome was a greater reminder than the coconuts of the reality of their return. Expelled for no reason that anyone could agree on, they arrived mainly by road, clutching patterned bags to their chests, in trucks hired by the Ghana government. They were mainly teachers and mechanics, a few musicians who were not part of Nigerian-led bands, dancers, nurses, traders – even doctors. They claimed to have lost everything; they said Ifako had been razed to the ground by bulldozers; their houses, their TVs, their VW Beetles were gone. In time, the bags they clutched would come to be known as Agege Sacks or Ghana Must Go bags. With their arrival, the food shortage turned acute. Hunger had arrived and it was staying for a while. It was for this reason that Naa Okailey was prepared to let her son go to Fumaz. The fates had willed that he was the one child the right age to go, the seed picked by the bird of chance.

In Fumaz, on Isla de la Inocencia, there was food – three times a day – and Yunior was grateful for that, regardless of what he thought of the barbed wire perimeter. He had been living on one full meal a day in Accra – without meat and often without even bones. He also preferred the uniform on Isla – burgundy shorts and a white shirt – a mirror of the buildings, which were painted burgundy on the lower halves of their walls.

And although he would not say it out loud, he was relieved to be able to make mistakes away from the surveillance of his mother, to escape what she called his *fear of things*. She had used those words intermittently since he was little, but the last time she had used them before he left Accra, he had been ashamed and truly fearful of what might have been. Walking from his school, he had passed a child playing at the foot of a neem tree about half a kilometre from his home. He paused to watch her, worried, but he thought that one of the people milling about must be with the child, so he carried on home. Still, the image of the child hovered in his mind like a persistent fly and his mother must have sensed this, because immediately after she hugged him on his return home, she held him away from her and asked, "What's wrong?"

"Nothing, Ma," Yunior shrugged, putting his bag down.

"My son, something is wrong, so tell me what it is you are telling me is nothing, because nothing is still a thing."

When he told her, she shook her head. "You see what I tell

you about your fear of things? Don't you know that in these times with no food, people can do what one is not supposed to do? Did you see someone watching over her?"

"Please, no."

"My child, Kole, I'm going to tell you this thing just once: everything is at home unless it is alone. Do you hear?"

"Please, yes."

"You will go back right now and if they are still there and nobody is watching them, you will bring the girl child home. Do you hear?"

Yunior had to skip school the next day, staying at home to look after the girl. His mother said that she would find the child's parents and he believed her; there was nothing you couldn't find out at the central market – especially if the traders trusted you. They were up before the first flap of the cock's wing to get their wares to the market and they were still in the streets when the bustle settled at night; they saw everything, and what they didn't see their customers told them about. So he washed the child and fed her and soothed her and waited, but he couldn't look the girl in the eyes.

He was not surprised when his mother came home with his little siblings, Jemima and Baby Nii, and a young woman who looked relieved and fearful at once. His mother ushered his siblings into the house to go and greet their father, and addressed the young woman on the verandah.

"So, this is where I live. When there is no food for the child, come to us. The little we have, we will share. It is not for food that we abandon a child. Have you forgotten how hard it is to bear a child?"

The woman shook her head, mumbling something inaudible as she shrank into the green and orange of the cloth wrapped around her chest.

Naa Okailey turned to her son. "Kole, give the child to their mother."

Yunior stood to hand her over, but the child clung to his neck and wouldn't let go, even when her mother reached out.

"What are they called?" he asked.

"Teki," said the girl's mother.

"Teki." Yunior hoisted the girl higher. "You have to go to your mother now."

The girl unwrapped her short, dark arms from Yunior's neck and held his face with her little hands, fingers spread across his cheeks, stared into his eyes, and smiled for the first time since he had picked her up from the side of the road.

When the woman had gone with her child, thanking Naa Okailey profusely as she left, Yunior's mother sighed.

She turned to her son. "You see how that child loves you? This fear of things you have, you need to leave it behind. People need people to see them. That girl is your first child."

She opened her arms. "Come."

When Yunior embraced her, she slapped his back. "Can you imagine what could have happened to the child?" Then she held her son for a long time, with leaves rustling in the darkness settling around them. It was still months before he left for Fumaz, but it felt like goodbye.

Because Yunior was as much an exile on our great green island country as his classmates, his stuttering Spanish found resonance within the enclosure they lived in. When there were breaks between lessons, Yunior's drumming on his desk drew in a coterie of rhythm-loving friends – a gap-toothed Angolan youth, Manjate, among the closest.

In time Yunior would answer more readily to Spanish than Ga or Twi; he would learn to play street baseball as the local youths did, wielding a bat with affected nonchalance; he would come to appreciate peopleist philosophy and spend his weekends helping younger children with their homework. With every passing year his body fell more easily into the rhythm of the local son music. When Profesor Hernandez, the man who had inadvertently renamed him, handed him an old guitar, Yunior's fingers sought and moulded themselves to the tension of acoustic strings. Through it he blended with the countryside – its fertility, its undulating earth, its cycles, the muted music of its flora flourishing and fading, its temper when hurricanes flashed nearby. Losing the city's pulse inside of him, he became a boy of the countryside – muchacho del campo – and his fellow students at Escuela Secondaria Basica en el Campo B – ESBEC B – became his comrades.

Although they dispersed like windblown silk cotton seeds after their secondary education, they kept in touch. Those who, like Yunior, had learned to play an instrument occasionally ran into each other at university music events, or at concerts in Aguana where their idols from Fumaz or neighbouring islands, such as Alberto Sanchez (who had been born not far from ESBEC B) and Elena Burke, were playing with big bands in which all the players were – to their ears – perfect. The rest remained connected by hearsay and letters, which were soon referring to shortages of canned goods from USSRs, which formed the basis of most diets in Fumaz. It became steadily clear to Yunior that they were heading for a food shortage like the one he had escaped in Ghana. But this shortage was different; in Ghana, deprived of water for months, the soil could not support new growth so the solutions had to come from outside their borders, or from adaptations of their diet. In Accra, instead of kontomire, which had all but disappeared with the cocoyams that formed its roots, they had begun to eat the bɔkɔbɔkɔ leaves that grew wild along walls, in the cracks that lined open gutters, down back streets where gangsters congregated to split their loot, and at the edges of wells that mocked searchers with reflections from their almost-empty depths. Here in Fumaz, the soil was fertile, there was rain and there was manpower, but for years they had only farmed en masse for export, in cooperatives that supplied government distributors, never planting to feed themselves. Even the farmers who might have dared to ignore the quota they were contracted to supply to the government were too scared to try crops that they had never grown before. Old habits died hard.

With his realisation of what was coming, by the time *half-time* arrived in 1991, Yunior, by now at the Universidad Agraria de Los Cien Vientos del Oeste, in Bana, Western Provinces, was already cultivating a plot of varied food crops. He had made arrangements with a nearby sugar-producing farm owned by the Gonzalez family to work a section of their plantation based on organic agricultural production methods, as the price for sugar began to drop. Once the real shortages set in by mid-1991, he was able to help the Gonzalez family and the neighbouring farms to switch their output from cash crops to local consumption crops.

It was not a straightforward process; most of the farmers were accustomed to the convenience of using tractors, combine harvesters and mechanised irrigation and struggled to adapt to manual methods. However, the decline of the USSRs economy and its subsequent division into new nations, meant that the petroleum that Fumaz used to get in exchange for its sugar was no longer forthcoming. The farmers had no choice. Stories of how their grandfathers used to farm became the order of the day as they trekked to and from wells and standpipes. To sell produce outside of Bana, the eleven horses in the town were called into action – haltered, saddled, bridled and attached to carts. Their crownpieces were pulled into place behind their ears, their breast collars checked, they were patted on the head, and put to work. But several of the farms, their soils impoverished by years of planting cane and sustaining volumes by using fertilisers, took years to produce a good harvest.

It was the Gonzalez men who told him the perennial joke about his name.

"Do you know what Yunior is?" asked, Julio, the father.

"Yeah, it's my name."

"No," Julio laughed, "it's the name of a one-night-stand. You know why?"

Yunior shook his head.

"There are so many Yuniors, and they are very hard to trace – unless you know the full name. So, when a girl is asked out and her date says he's called Yunior, we assume he just wants a good time – there's no plan beyond one-night, for how would she trace him?"

This is how on Yunior's first visit to Aguana to play in a live band, he was able to tell the joke to the drummer, one of only two native Fumazero in the quintet, whose brother shared Yunior's name. Warming up absent-mindedly, his hardened fingertips skimming the guitar strings, he overheard the man lamenting how his brother, resentful of the way Guerrero Rosario's policies had curtailed their wealthy family's influence, had migrated to the USAs.

Yunior cut in with the joke and added, "At least over there his name may be less of a code and more of an identity." He extended his hand. "I'm also Yunior, by the way. By accident, but that's my name now."

"Marcos," the drummer replied. "Manjate told me a lot about you, Yunior. You sing as well, yes? Like a Fumazero."

"I am Fumazero."

BANA

Marcos was the reason why Yunior started taking food from his farm to Aguana at the height of *half-time*. It was never planned; it just happened once and grew into something that was expected.

The quintet Yunior played in with Marcos, Los Puntos Estelares, was offered a fortnightly slot at one of the leading salsa clubs, Verde, a place where, regardless of local conditions, foreigners still visited and spent good money on alcohol, cigars and the promise of love. Knowing the difficulty of getting good food in Aguana once the supply from USSRs had dried up, Yunior travelled to the two-night engagements of Los Puntos Estelares with some basic supplies for himself – three carrots, a head of cabbage, two red onions and a handful of frijoles negros that swelled to three times their original size when soaked overnight. Vegetables and legumes – vitamins and protein. The first time Yunior travelled east, mindful that Marcos had a young daughter, he harvested an identical mix of vegetables for him, making a mental note to add some frijoles from the sack he kept on his kitchen table. Then, surveying his half-acre plot, its boundary marked by a thigh-high chicken run that held six clucking red- and brown-feathered hens, Yunior shrugged and uprooted carrots and onions for his other band mates. Peopleist philosophy was now almost instinctive. While there was fresh food in the countryside, the city, with its benign cancers of hotels and tourists, was another story.

In a break during rehearsals, Yunior handed drummer, trumpeter, pianist and bass player roughly-cut sugar sacks sewn into quaint, small bags with spirals of twine.

Marcos, having opened his makeshift bag, stared at its contents almost without recognition, then he jumped up to fold Yunior in a bear hug. "I haven't seen cabbage for so long, brother. So long."

The rest of the band converged on Yunior, mumbling their appreciation and light-heartedly describing the wonderful meals they were going to cook, until they heard Marcos's bass drum ringing with the beat of their first song. They still had to rehearse.

Yunior took his position in front of the quintet and prepared to sing their signature song, "Vivimos Juntos". He lifted his guitar strap over his head and as he lowered it onto his left shoulder, he noticed his shirt was wet with Marcos's tears.

After Yunior started adding eggs to the rations he packed for his band mates, he was approached by the owner of Verde about supplying produce to his brother's grocery store on a side street close by.

"I don't produce much," said Yunior. "Only a half-acre, and I only come here twice a month."

"It's OK. Even a little will be helpful to the locals."

Gente had already lost the right to be called a grocery store. Its shelves swept bare by the lack of imports from USSRs and the direct-to-hotel trade of fresh produce, it had only a supply of locally-produced cigars in a cabinet to the right of the till. The shelves, painted in alternate greens and yellows, borrowed from the same palette that created the Fumazero flag, looked like wings shed by small planes that had lost the desire to fly. Flor and Tomas, the owners, had kept the store open by taking in laundry from the same hotels that had severed the lines of vegetable supply from the farmers. Their son sat on the floor in the back, drawing clouds with his foot on a bag of dirty linen that had just arrived. In fact, Gente had become a launderette disguised as a place where one could go and buy food, and it remained a launderette after Yunior arrived with his first delivery.

"You won't display the vegetables?"

"No," explained Flor, her dark lips spreading into a smile. "We cannot sell like this. It is not official. We will tell the people at home and they will come."

Boxes of onions, potatoes, carrots, cabbages, lettuce and tomatoes were packed in a back room and, before Yunior left, he was relieved to see a bare-chested boy walk in with a note for Flor, hand over a clutch of pesos, and leave with a bag of potatoes, onions and a head of cabbage.

Yunior charged Flor and Tomas no more for the vegetables than he made at government-backed produce markets in the Western Provinces. They only had to cover the extra cost of his transporting the 100 kilo assortment of vegetables by horse and the converted military trucks that ferried hordes of people along the same route that Western Provinces traders, such as Diego Soñada Santos, used to build their empires of influence.

Every kilometre they now travelled had once had ruts bitten and carved into earth by carriage wheels of wood and steel, and these roads were themselves the descendants of narrow paths turned wide and hardened by tramping feet. Carts and carriages laden with goats, rice, maize, wheat, various grades of sugar, cattle, chickens, potatoes, a colourful range of fruits, ducks, pigs and leather hides had all rumbled along this route, bringing profit to early trading families. In his journeys, Yunior was living the very supply chain he had read about in course books. Of course, back then, canoes and river steamers had also played a part in getting livestock and grain from the more remote farms to the browning swathes that were cut by horsemen and foot travellers through the countryside's green ebullience. With only one kilometre of narrow gauge railway per 3600 inhabitants in the early 1900s, roads and rutted paths had remained the primary mode of transport for traders.

When Yunior travelled from Bana for performances with Los Puntos Estelares, he would spend the journey reading up on food processing and animal husbandry in the seminal text, *Plantation Economies of Fumaz*, and he still dedicated spare hours in the city to reading theses on crop rotation, subsidence and the long-term effects of fertiliser use and papers on efficient farm-layout, and the wild medicinal herbs that were threatened by large-scale agriculture and low-cost irrigation.

He was still a student; he had no time to visit produce markets in Aguana, so he wasn't aware that vegetables, when available, fetched far higher prices in the city than he was charging. When the locals, who still saw him dipping in and out of the shade of the city's trees, delivering crates and sacks to Gente, stopped waving at him and calling out *hermano*, he failed to noticed. The growing flamboyance of Tomas's striped shirts and the sparkle of Flor's new shoes when they visited Verde to dance, didn't catch his eyes. Yunior loved seeing them happy and embraced them with customary exuberance, sharing in the laughter that lit their eyes like diamonds.

Flor often held his face and kissed him on the lips, ruffling his growing Afro. "Twenty-two. So hard-working, so good-looking. It's a pity we don't have a daughter for you." Tomas punched his arm and they all laughed. He didn't know that Flor and Tomas had stopped selling vegetables to all but their closest friends, that they were taking deliveries from him and reselling the produce to the hotels that glowed like enemy posts in Aguana nights – hotels that paid ten times the price Yunior charged Flor and Tomas.

When Yunior was leaving the club one evening, a dark woman with loose black curls that tumbled to the shoulder of the clinging red dress she wore, grasped his arm and followed him outside.

"Hi, I'm Loretta."

He was stunned, both by her radiance and her forwardness. "Yunior."

"Do you have something with that woman?" She jerked her head towards the door of Verde, still holding on to his left arm, her low heels keeping beat with his strides.

"Flor? No." He flashed an amused smile. "Are you jealous?"

"You are her business partner?"

Yunior frowned at the turn the conversation had taken. "No. I sell vegetables to her store sometimes. She is a friend."

Loretta stepped up to walk ahead of him and mumbled, "Come with me."

Yunior's frown eased into a grimace of realisation. His first encounter with the secret police.

Following Loretta into a Spanish-style villa turned dull by night, Yunior was ushered into what must once have been a lavatory where a young man in tan trousers, a green t-shirt and a cap as flat as his expression, informed him that they had been observing the counter-revolutionary activities of Flor and Tomas for five months.

They had started in May 1991, nine months earlier, when Yunior first delivered vegetables to Gente.

"So this is an interrogation?" Yunior asked.

The flat cap glanced at Loretta who shook her head so slightly that it almost didn't happen.

"No," said flat cap. "We are just confirming information. We halted observation after a month because the locals said that they were able to get affordable produce from the shop."

Yunior exhaled, feeling his sweat from the club drying on his skin.

The man continued. "In September, an old lady complained that vegetables were no longer available, although they still saw you arriving with sacks and crates twice a month."

Loretta took over, looking out of place with her red dress and mildly dishevelled hair. "We went to Bana and saw the good work you are doing there with the farmers. The Universidad say you are a brilliant student too."

Yunior nodded, finally leaning back in the low chair he had been given.

"We just had to be sure that you weren't involved in the black market trade with the hotels like Flor and Tomas."

He was to say nothing about this conversation as Loretta would be observing the Gente operation for another month to identify all the counter-revolutionaries. The Agriculture Minister was interested in his organic farming work in Bana and the smaller project he had started recently on a visit to Isla de la Inocencia. He would accompany the minister to Bana to look more closely at his farm.

It was in the Agriculture Minister's jeep, the minister's long arm reaching across him to point, that Yunior first saw the Soñada Santos rice estate in Asadon.

"The owner is a good supporter of the revolution. The family gave half of their land to the local peasants after our liberation in 1959," said the minister, pushing his sunglasses further up his nose.

"It doesn't look very productive," Yunior said, taking in the estate's vast, ordered but sickly-looking rice paddies and imposing avenue of mahogany trees leading up a slight incline to a centrally-placed grand house.

"True. I think their yield has been falling for years, but it doesn't matter. The rice from here is worth its weight in gold – it's the sweetest rice in Fumaz. They export 90% of their output to gourmet restaurants around the world."

"So how do they sell so well? What's their secret?"

The Agriculture Minister shrugged his military shoulders.

"There are many stories. The most popular is that there are sugar pipes under the ground. But the workers don't talk – they all live on the land. They are like a family."

Yunior fell silent and remained so as they approached Bana. Trees crept closer and closer to the road until they were driving under a canopy of green. Wild guava, simaruba, breadfruit, clusters of jocuma blanca with attila birds weaving their white-yellow bellies between them, drooping mangoes, citrus, large jabillo and broad leaves of papaya hung above them. A fertile smell of fruit and fungus, a muted hum of rot and renewal, enveloped them. A single shaft of sunlight that split the road in two marked their route all the way to Bana.

The buzz of excitement that accompanied their arrival brought back to Yunior recollections of the early days of Jerry Rawlings' ascent to power in Ghana, when the Head of State used to turn up unannounced and initiate area cleaning exercises. It also reminded Yunior of his first months on the isla, the mania that accompanied his football exploits. However, as the minister introduced himself to a wizened but wiry farmer, who smiled warily, and questioned him about the new farming system, the balance of crops that they had chosen to cultivate, Yunior's mind kept drifting back to the Soñada Santos rice estate, especially the house up the incline: a canary-yellow building gone pale with neglect, though its faded white stilts still looked solid, its large windows like pale-rimmed eyes begging for attention. Surrounding it was almost every ornamental tree he had ever studied on the entire island of Fumaz, including his favourite, the majestic imperial palm. In the wooden interior of the house he could imagine the resonance of laughter and song, the syncopation of footsteps in dance. The estate seemed to him a place where love and indulgence should reign.

All through his distracted reverie, Yunior remained aware that the minister's questioning of the gathered denizens was engineered to serve the unspoken purpose of this visit, to check his story, making sure that he actually did the work he claimed to do in the community. There was clearly a concern that he should have no connection whatsoever with the black market operation his friends in Aguana were involved in.

Tomas and Flor had been escorted quietly away from Gente one morning, with Yunior brought along to confirm, with a most awkward nod, that he supplied them with fresh produce. They avoided his eyes as their son, who was playing in the back room, was carried out in the arms of a woman who looked like she would rather be tackling an armed criminal to the ground. She was kindly looking with a hint of steel in the flex of her brow. Dressed in a blue skirt and yellow blouse, she rubbed the boy's back, whispering, "Calmate niño, calmate mijo, calmate."

Yunior had gone through six sessions of interrogation – covering everything from his sleeping habits to his guitar-playing hobby – before this trip with the minister. He was tempted to feel offended that his story was still being vetted; instead, a bubble of orange joy bloomed in his chest as the minister finally loosened up and asked him about his favourite salsa songs, the son musicians he liked, his favourite baseball players – even adding surreptitiously, "and in the USAs?" – before revealing that he, too, played the guitar and would come and sit in at one of Yunior's performances sometime.

By the time Yunior had returned to his small piece of Bana earth, surveyed his half-acre plot, checked on his dozen chickens and taken off his shoes to relax in the hammock he hung between two poles in the square arch that divided the kitchen from the living quarters, the bubble of joy had filled his cheeks with a satisfied smile. He had been questioned about everything one could possibly do wrong in Fumaz, and at no stage had he been asked for his passport. He had been considered a native. He was rooted, embedded, he was

Fumazero. The rain beginning to fall outside was his; it would fall on his land, his plants, make them grow.

AGUANA

Operating from his half-acre haven in Bana after completing his studies at Los Cien Vientos, Yunior worked for the government as an agricultural consultant, with responsibility for converting long-established monoculture farms into more vibrant, multi-crop operations to better serve the needs of Guerrero Rosario's people. He was one of a group of former students employed as Oficiales de Divulgación para el Cambio (ODC). Their job was to convince families that had cultivated sugar cane, vetiver, coffee and tobacco for generations, to yield their land to a mixed basket of frijoles, corn, peppers, sweet potatoes, cereals, onions and squashes. It was a task that took delicacy, a fine balance of negotiation and persuasion that tasked the tongue's ability to manoeuvre round bitter twists.

As he walked down each path, under clusters of green that provided shade to assemblies of families massed into walls of defiance, Yunior hummed Elena Burke songs, or, lately, snippets from songs revived by the new phenomenon from their Cuban island neighbours, The Buena Vista Social Club. He did it to stay loose, to keep his tongue supple. Once in front of the families, he unleashed his full smile and set loose his fast-talking patter, expressing himself with larger than required gestures, creating images to excite the imaginations of his listeners. For him, farming was akin to magic – it held the power to transform not just the look of land, but the lives of the people who lived on it. And some kinds of farming could be harmful – the loss of wildlife species in places like India and

South Africa was not just due to trophy hunting, but also aggressive large-scale agriculture that had destroyed the habitats of animals like quagga and dwarf rhinos. And in Fumaz, if they kept planting sugarcane at a time when they needed potatoes to eat, they would eventually die.

"La mala agricultura es la muerte," he would exclaim, his enthusiasm bubbling over.

The families could tell that he genuinely wanted to help and that was why he was one of the most successful ODC of the Ministry of Agriculture's task force. Add to that the guitar that clung to his back like an orphan fearful of abandonment, and the almost universal Fumazero love for music, for rhythm, for dancing, and you can understand why the man was so successful. Once his official duties were done, Yunior was quick to free the well-travelled guitar from his back and coax son notes from its stringed neck. An abuelo would disappear indoors, emerge with a cajón, and music would invade the air, sending signals via butterflies, birds and bats to summon the darkness home – a song at night, a farm transformed.

By 1997, food production for domestic consumption had improved dramatically, cereal yield per hectare was up by quarter of a tonne, but there remained the problem of transporting food from the provinces to the cities in a country with so little fuel. The spectre of spoilage in Fumaz's humid heat meant that horses were not a practical solution; they were too slow, too convenient for the life aspirations of micro-organisms. So the focus turned to supporting the emerging trend of urban farming via a Rosario government initiative, to which Yunior was assigned, returning him to the city where his work first brought him to the attention of the government. He was to help elevate the harvests of the city's denizens beyond subsistence levels, so that Aguana could be sustained by its own output – it was the logical next step.

In the peopleist spirit, Yunior himself kept a garden on the roof of the building where he lived on Calle 41. There had been a couple of old ornamental plants that he mostly cleared, repurposing the area for food crops. Gardening in the city was different from keeping a half-acre plot on a fertile countryside estate; gardening on a rooftop was a world with an entire vocabulary of its own. Getting soil up to his roof, protecting germinating seeds from the loud Aguana sun and keeping roots moist in a space without natural shade took swear, defiance and single-minded faith. But Yunior knew what he was doing. Rotating peppers, spring onions, tomatoes, sweet potatoes and cabbages with assorted frijoles, okra, red onions, cucumbers, lettuce and aubergines, he prided himself on a garden that was both colourful and nutritious. He often sat on the roof after tending to his small cuadrado verde, staring at the Aguana sky's festival of changing colours and catching strains of music floating up from the nearby school of ballet and clusters of musicians rehearsing on wide avenues. When the gentle slap of the nearby ocean raised itself to a rhythm of crashing and wild volleys of spray, he would rise and peer over roofs towards the coast, the Malecón snaking along the contours of their beautiful island, colourful cars following the road's darkening path.

With the pace at which he had to learn when he arrived in Fumaz and his own parents' admonishment to focus, Yunior had eased his childhood into a distant corner of his memory, where it sat, only occasionally seeping into his consciousness. He had sent letters home to mark the important milestones – copies of his certificates after each stage of study, a picture of his graduation from Universidad Agraria de Los Cien Vientos del Oeste and the letter confirming his first job with the government of Fumaz; in return, he had one new picture of his siblings from 1987 and three letters: the first to thank God for his safe arrival in Fumaz and tell him to focus; the second (which came with the picture of his siblings) to inform him of the death of his mother's cousin who helped look after him when he was a baby; the third to send him a newspaper clipping of himself coming top of his class on graduation in Fumaz – news that had somehow made the front page of the *Ghanaian Times*.

Like the other ESBEC students, he did not come from a family that could pay for a flight back home for a holiday. They had arrived on government funding and it would be up to the government to decide who returned and when. He'd learned to suppress nostalgia to a point where it had become second nature, but on nights like this, with the sea nudging the shore as it did in Accra, the palms swaying like their cousins on the West African coast, Yunior would let out a sigh.

Acknowledging kindred night-gazing rooftop neighbours with a quick 'hola', before heading down to his flat he'd caress the stem of the lone sunflower that stood in his congregation of food plants. Huddled in the shadow of a gnarled miniature olive tree he barely took notice of, it was a burst of yellow indulgence that brought him great pleasure. He missed his half-acre in Bana, now cared for by the Gonzalez family; perhaps he missed his own family's mango tree in Ghana, but the plants on his roof were closer to him.

Yunior was not the only one planting in joy and the quest for balanced meals. Persuaded by Rosario-sanctioned incentives and by the outreach work he and his team had done in the city, by 1998 there were 9,320 of the four types of cuadrados verdes in Aguana, using many rooftops, balconies and patches of undeveloped city land. Many of the number were, like Yunior's, huertos populares, small gardens grown by households to suit their particular tastes and diets. At work, he also directed the Empresas Estatales cuadrados verdes, which were much more than squares – large areas of government-held urban farmland which also served as research bases for Yunior and his colleagues to experiment on good organic farming practices that they distilled into tips to pass on to every kind of urban farmer. Yunior considered the research a kind of apprenticeship in spreading love on the planet: putting crops from different backgrounds together to benefit from each other's strengths; creating conducive, manured environments for them to be fruitful; drafting in nitrogen-fixing beans to enhance fertility; soliciting the help of flowers to attract insects that eliminate pests; and crowding out weeds by sticking cultivated plants closer together. They experimented with collecting worms and immersing them in less fertile soils to enhance the quality of the soil through aeration and higher levels of organic activity. They learned how to seduce ants with honey-coated plantain peels placed in sweet potato fields – once in the fields, the ants consumed the parasites that loved to bore through the flesh of the sweet potatoes. It was rewarding work because barely anything had to be bought – it just took the farmer's effort.

With the fortieth anniversary of the Rosario revolution coming, there was more urgency to everyone's work, for no country wants to turn forty without being able to fend for itself. Yunior's band mates from Los Puntos Estelares were also in Aguana, but they were all so caught up with work that they only played quarterly.

Marcos was involved in social welfare research, observing the lives of a group of senior citizens and recording their diets, exercise regimes, and health indicators in a joint project with the Aguana Medical School. This had finished in mid-1998, and he was due to deliver the report shortly. Manjate, in spite of civil war in his native Angola, was involved in an initiative to source oil for Fumaz from Luanda. George and Esperanza were both working at full tilt as medical doctors.

It was a real battle to keep up their composition and performance with all the work that they had to do to further the Fumazero dream. Recently, they had been courted by offers. Because of the success of the Buena Vista Social Club and Omega Aventura in Europe and USAs, they had been approached by festival directors and producers from USAs, Canada and Europe inviting them to be a young Buena Vista, but the proposals didn't feel right.

When they met and played, their music had new textures because of their engagement with the sweat and fears of the land. Their pauses were more knowing from their dance with the hopes and indomitable dreams that trickle down the backs of the people and gather into one stream, one river, one salt-free gush into the sea of future possibilities.

In the dance schools the children still leap, in the public squares the abuelos and abuelas stretch and dance, and hunger's shadow is not big enough to obscure the sun. It may be *half-time*, but there is a new time being born in the fat bottoms of city aubergines, in the shaker music of shelled frijoles, in the city centre clock that a cluster of engineering students scale a sheer wall to fix with no authorisation from the government – an act that Guerrero Rosario, in his weekend speech, cannot decide whether to condemn as nonconformist or praise as pioneering. In the end, he simply names it an act of peopleism, a response to the need of the city's people to know what time it is. He tugs on the furthest point of his waterfall beard that he can reach; this is contemplation, these are the struggles of ageing revolutionaries.

And, as the fortieth anniversary of the revolution nears and Rosario renews himself by having his beard braided like a swarthy fairytale hero, there are signs that *half-time* may be passing, that it may finally be Fumazero time. Marcos's report is one of the first well-researched markers: there have been significant declines in deaths attributed to diabetes, stroke and coronary heart disease among the elderly.

Elsewhere, researchers have found that 80% of our fauna population – human and non-human, including rats – are receiving their daily calorific requirements from the harvests. The people have already felt it in their stomachs, but it is nice to hear Rosario proclaim, "Camaradas, hemos venido a través del fuego. Nuestras luchas fueron fructíferas. *Half-time* is over!"

The news rides the wind, bristles on our leaves, takes shape on televisions, in radios, in the newspapers held in hands to swat flies with. But let our joys not distract us from the real story.

The improved fortunes of Fumaz lead Los Puntos Estelares to finally accept an invitation to play abroad. Of course, they refuse the name the USAs marketing guru comes up with, Jóvenes Machotes de Verde, a name that seems to want to sell them like that male stripper group, The Chippendales, completely ignoring Esperanza's presence and contribution. What band can play well without a steady hand at the double bass, without the resonant fidelity of that curved wood? So, because of the nature of the USAs man's badly-washed character, they travel, not to the USAs, but to Jamaica to play their first shows away from Fumaz.

Their four of performances in January 1999, in the wake of the Jazz Jamaica Festival held just a month before, were a grand success. Arriving too late for the festival in Ocho Rios, and featuring world-class stars such as Chaka Khan, Baaba Maal and guitar great George Benson, Los Puntos Estelares were originally scheduled to play two nights at the private retreat of a record producer, also in Ocho Rios. However, the tumultuous reception of the performance of their signature, "Vivimos Juntos", a song that resonated so strongly with Jamaica's own national motto "Out of Many, One People", led to a hasty arrangement with an international hotel in Montego Bay to host them for two nights. Music journalists, heralding the band for its infectious dance rhythms, the casual professionalism of the musicians and the strange familiarity of their neighbour-sound, were happy to have public dates to recommend to their readers.

Rehearsing to the backdrop of a bleeding sunset, Marcos turned to Yunior, "Long way from the start of *half-time*, hermano, eh?"

"Very long way. Very long... But we are almost there."

"It was a genius idea to say the lyrics in English before the solos, George – estupendo!!

They were spoiled. Attendants fussed over their every need. Yunior, George and Marcos had kept to themselves, but Esperanza and Manjate were pursued by eligible men and women in this playground of Jamaica's rich and the international elite. A spread of salads, boiled roots, spicy fish and chicken, octopus, rice and desserts, had been constantly available. In the hotel gift shops, they were dazzled by the expensive jewellery, slick clothes and alcohol. But Manjate noted how the cigars that they took for granted in Fumaz attracted exorbitant prices here.

"I would rather drink and smoke for less, my friends. I am a simple man," he said.

Yunior, speaking English again for the first time in a decade and a half, began to feel stirrings to visit his mother, his father, and the younger siblings he barely knew.

It was Esperanza who asked the question they all had in their minds. They had never been due to receive so much money before.

"What will we do with the money?"

George and Manjate spoke as one. "Send it home."

"Sudan is hard, but there are some good changes coming. The money will help my parents," George added.

"I'll try to buy a place in Aguana," Marcos said. "Leave something solid for the kids."

"You?" Esperanza turned to Yunior, peering over a banana milkshake. She held the stem of the glass with the same assured grasp she used for her double bass.

Yunior paused, catching her eyes. "I think I'm going to take some time off after our visit to Montreal; go and see my family in Accra."

"How many years?" she asked.

"Fifteen – almost sixteen."

"Seventeen," said George, "seventeen."

"Can I say something?" said Esperanza. "It's not very peopleist, but I want a swimming pool. Like this one." She stood, shedding a monogrammed hotel towel and dived into clear blue water.

Fumaz is blue hills kissing an orange sky, where tobacco grows that dries as red as blood. The barks of the trees carry ingrown messages from rebels who sheltered in our forests, battled the Spaniards, Portuguese, USAs, frustrated the neo-colonialists and toppled the USAs-backed Capitalites. If you run your hand along the rough of a tree's history and close your eyes, you will see Mambí-inspired young men crawling through the undergrowth, sheltering under umbrella canopies, measuring gunpowder, sharpening makeshift arrows, buttressing their courage with sips of the fermented fruits of the forest; you will hear the emergence of radio waves, the slip of combatants closer to the villages that have replaced clusters of trees, feel the feverish, doomed love that grows between these green-black-clad men and the girls that hide their guns and fetch water for them to drink. There are offspring in the offing. The entire nation was born between the soil and those trees. If you plunge your hand into the soil, raise it to your nose and smell it, the land will dwell in your heart forever. When you leave, it will turn your face bitter; when you return, it will fill your cheeks with light.

Emelina Santos has grown up with these stories. The myth of Fumaz – received by whispers through spoonfuls of six-hour-soft frijoles infused with garlic, pork and red onions and mixed with saffron rice and from the torque of her mother's centrifugal embrace – resides beneath her tongue. Where her father Juan's memories were the vague images of a seven-year-old, her mother's were vivid, intricate canvasses awash with longing. It was the longing of a twelve-year-old who had lost her mother to heartbreak, a death from causes unknown, but which had its roots in the disappearance of her one true love, Gabo. He had left no message for her; all that remained of him was the child, Emelina's mother, whom he named Alae. She was five when he left. She could not remember him, but after he has gone, the stories began.

He was in love with a woman named Alae before he met the child's mother. She was dark, she was light, she was kind, she was mean, she was calculating, she was sincere, she had rejected him, he had resisted her. It was hard to know what was true. What was true was that Alae's mother loved Gabo with all her heart, loved him as much as the soil she was born on; that he held her and looked her in the eye every night and made love to her, that he wrapped himself in her dark skin as morning came; that if he ever showed signs of being unhappy she blamed herself. She asked what she could do, she even asked if he wanted to be free of her. What was true was that he left one afternoon to buy bread and never returned, and in seven years Alae's mother was reduced to dust.

No doctor could heal her, no soothsayer could soothe her and no rumour could make her understand how her heart could give so much love and be left bereft. If her family could celebrate the report of Gabo dying in a bar fight after *his* Alae betrayed him, it only made her hurt more. She loved him and, in spite of the hurt, she wanted him to be happy – not heartbroken, not dead. But there was no stopping her own decline, and the dark soil she loved to clasp in her palms was soon in the hands of her daughter who, racked by tears, tossed them on top of the wood of her coffin. With Gabo untraceable, Alae was adopted by her mother's younger sister, Susie, who raised her in the village of blue hills, the land that had nurtured the family for generations.

But these tales are not fairy-forged, so I don't have to tell you that there is sour in their sweet. Susie soon met a man of her own, Vincente; he was one of those who had decided that Fumaz was not where his future lay – it was across the seas to USAs. Susie's heart was hooked and stretched and split. Between her love of this land, high in the east of Fumaz, where the tobacco dries like blood, and her yearning for this man who made her entire body burst into flames, she was unhinged. Her pondering had her walking the land, her feet bare, drawing noughts and crosses across the soil. There was never going to be a winner. Preoccupied, she didn't notice Vincente's tourist eyes, how they liked to settle on the fourteen-year-old Alae. It took Susie a year to decide she would move with him.

Yes, Emelina's mother's stories were imbued with the longing of a child forced to leave a land she loves, to become a woman before her time. They will hold you captive even if they do not break your heart; their longing will bind you with restlessness.

The first time he touches her, it is like an accident. He reaches past her to grab a beer from the fridge and his arm brushes her left breast. Tía Susie is right beside him, but Alae catches a look in his eye that makes her uncomfortable. She is not naïve; she has heard the girls talk in high school – the things men do to try to turn you on; what to do if you want to ride in a Ford convertible; how to look after yourself at the make-out spot; how to snag a cool guy. He could easily have asked her to pass him the beer.

The second time, there is no mistaking his motive. He 'squeezes' past her while she is ironing; she can feel his hard penis through his pants and there is plenty of space in the laundry room. She turns with the iron held high and he flees, laughing.

She tells Tía Susie, but her aunt is too in love to believe her, calls her ungrateful. She points to her Cynthia Robinson inspired afro, accuses Alae of being misled by her friends, trying to unsettle her marriage. Her rage rustles the leaves of the Sun Coast's flora.

"Will you stop at nothing to move back to Fumaz?"

Alae is stunned, but there is little she can do to convince Tía Susie.

When Vincente next catches her alone, it is clear Tía Susie has told him about her complaint. He is unrepentant. "Nowhere to run, nowhere to hide," he whispers, placing his finger under her chin, then walking away.

For months, Alae's life becomes a game of cat and mouse. Vincente is unrelenting and Tía Susie can't see anything with clarity. She is working two jobs and perfecting her English. She is often too tired to do much except watch TV, with Vincente caressing her back and staring at Alae. The school nurse, also from Fumaz, notices Alae's change in demeanour and invites her for coffee.

"¿Azúcar?" she asks.

It is not for us to know if it was the tone of her voice, or the fact that she asked Alae in the language of the land she has left, the land she misses so much, or if it was the nurse's skin, dark as her mother's, or the gap between her front teeth, as prominent as her grandfather's, but Alae cries as the whole story comes tumbling out as the nurse holds her face against her ample chest.

"You don't have to stay, ya sabes? This is not like Fumaz where we solve everything at home; you should report to the school; they will help you get a shelter."

Alae feels like a stone that suddenly has wings. "I can leave?"

"Yes. I even know someone from home at the Sun Coast Bridge Center – I can ask…"

"But my Tía…?"

"You can still see her. You will just be away from the house."

One of the young men who volunteers at the Bridge Center on weekends is also from Fumaz. When he speaks to the migrants who gather for free food in the evenings, he speaks a Spanish that has the music of the streets of USAs. The migrants are from Honduras, Nicaragua, the Dominican Republic and Fumaz. Newly arrived, they look haggard, but their gazes burn with determination. The young man looks them in the eye as he dishes out rice before they move along to Alae, who also works there, to serve vegetables. To her he only speaks English. He looks at her from the side of his angular face, but rarely engages in conversation. It is over a year later, on her seventeenth birthday, that he finally speaks to her in Spanish – to ask her out. Club 4381, the famous disco club, has started a teen night on Fridays and his cousin is working the door. Would she like to come for her birthday?

"¿Cómo sabes mi cumpleaños?"

"I talk to people, cariño. I ask questions." He smiles, then adds, "Sly and the Family Stone might be there tonight."

"And what if I have other plans?"

"The dance floor is wooden."

She laughs. Everyone knows the Fumazero love to dance on wood.

His name is Juan Soñada Santos. She already knows this, but he tells her anyway. His family own a chain of shops on the Sun Coast, but their wealth derives mainly from sales of a sweet rice grown on their family farm in Fumaz. When he speaks, she notes the gentle movements of his hands. His African ancestry is not obvious, but she traces it in the undertone of his skin, the kinks in his hairline, the tremulant bass of his laugh.

These are the stories that fire Emelina Santos's love of the homeland she has never visited. Between her mother's tobacco and her father's rice, she has grown up in the enchantment of music blaring from speakers every weekend, the unimprisonable aroma of fresh ground coffee drowned in milk and sugar, the lingering whispers from her father's celebratory cigars, her mother's fast, blunt Spanish, with its fading consonants.

When her grandfather, Elián, summons her to his home during her midwinter recess from college in February, she is puzzled. The old man prefers to call on her father unexpectedly, as though still testing his son; they rarely visit his home, up on a hill near where the Sun Coast peninsula connects to the mainland.

Elián watches her advance up the flagstone walkway and embraces her as he leads her past the aged, dark blue door that he had someone smuggle in from Aguana twenty-seven years ago, years before her birth. Her abuelo may have disagreed with his brother Ernesto about the value of Guerrero Rosario's peopleist approach and the merits of staying in Fumaz, but he had carried everything Fumazero that could be carried with him. If the storms had been portable, he would have travelled with them.

He keeps his arm around her as they walk to an open seating area with ochre tiles and a profusion of plant pots. "Mi vida, it is good to see you."

"It is always good to see you, Tata."

Elián makes a great show of letting her sit first, before he lowers himself beside her in the swinging seat. Emelina notices that he moves a little slower than he did when she last saw him. He holds himself with pride, his grey hair perfectly groomed, his eyes still keen and mischievous, but somehow his years are beginning to tell. It is almost as though a sadness is seeping into his bones.

"I have a message from your abuelo, Ernesto." Elián holds her hands in his as he tells her, as though afraid of delivering the message. "You know, my brother in…"

"I know who he is, Tata. What is the message?"

Her grandfather smiles. "He thinks you look like our grandmother. I sent him a picture." He pauses. "I can see it now. You have her smile, her smooth, dark skin…"

Elián stares at Emelina's hands as though trying to remember a moment in the past. A range of emotions play across his face, then he sighs. "I didn't offer you something to drink…"

Emelina shakes her head. "I'm OK."

He lets go of her hands and gestures towards the sky through the full length windows leading to a small garden. "They want you to go to Fumaz for my father's 99th birthday." He pauses. "Would you like to go?"

There is no hesitation from Emelina. "Yes."

"Are you sure? You have never been there."

She nods.

"You don't have to," Elián adds. "He is an old man; he won't really remember."

"But I want to. I have wondered about Fumaz all my life."

The light from outside frames Elián. He looks smaller, more frail – a crooked smile hangs across his face. He has been away from Fumaz for 37 years, longer than he lived there. He throws his arms open to embrace his granddaughter. "You were named for her, sabes?" he says. "Emelina Soñada. She was wonderful."

This is how Emelina Santos first visits Aguana. An invitation from her great-grandfather, Diego Soñada Santos, the man who with one stroke of sugar-laced inspiration altered the rice map of Fumaz, great-grandson of the liege of Luchando, that dog of a pig that laid the foundation of the family's fortunes. Once in Fumaz, what was myth will become flesh, will sing and dance and sweat before her. The familiarity, the heart-breaking catch in the music will make her knees buckle as she walks littered back streets; the formal postures of the old folk will remind her of her tata's measured walk; in the tight buns the women wear to tame their curly hair, she will find her mother's cross-border yearning.

She will arrive via Jamaica as there are no direct flights from the Sun Coast. Because of her arrival on March 28, 1999 – a Sunday – she will miss some college classes, but she is a sophomore, she knows how to keep up with a course when you have missed lectures. Besides, she will only be in Fumaz for a week; she will fly back on Friday, the morning after the party. When she returns to the Sun Coast she will graduate, she will go to law school, her life plan will not change.

For now, it is her arrival that counts. She will be met at the airport by her abuelo, Ernesto, who looks at least fifteen years younger than Tata. He will tell her to call him Lito, before regaling her with tales all the way to the old store house by the Malecón. Tales that make the streets break into alleyways and sprout touts, slick pickpockets, traders, spiralling dancers, half-blind spies, musicians, long-uprooted trees and endangered livestock – all in the storied, time-riddled garb of the real Aguana Vieja – ramped and massed against and between the old stone and wooden buildings that gave the city its music, its resonance. These were the streets her ancestors walked; this was the salt-charged air they dreamed in; that is the sun they watched fade to nothing, giving way to nights of love.

ACCRA

The Accra Yunior returned to was no longer under a haze of brown, no longer under military rule. From the air, the coastline was lavish with foam and tenacious clusters of flora. Sun glinted off the undulations of sea water. There was green everywhere, even encroaching into the city centre. He knew immediately that he would not be eating the rogue foods that sustained them in 1983, but with his experience from Fumaz, he wondered if those hardy plants should not be incorporated into everyday diets. Embarrassingly abundant wild copses of Madras thorn fruit and breadnut fruit could transform the diets of some of Accra's poorer akutsei. Yet he still dreamed of his mother's rich palaver sauce, its decadent red palm oil, its proud green kontomire, almost gone black in cooking and the contrast of carefully ground, pale agusi granules, like stars in that firmament of flavour.

He had changed too. He realised that when he was addressed as Oswald at the airport's entry counter and he barely responded. Even the sharp Twi accent of the immigration officer, a music he loved, now sounded mildly alien to him. He marked how much more humid it was in Accra than Aguana, how swiftly sweat gathered on his brow as he collected his suitcases.

When he had fitted his bags into the front boot and the back seat of the pale blue VW Beetle his father was driving, he turned to hug him again. Oswald Snr had filled out in his advanced years, his grey hairs lending him an aura of quiet authority, though he had to reach up to embrace his son, who had grown to a height he was not accustomed to.

"So, the car. When?" Yunior asked his father in Ga, weighing the language on his tongue. "When you wrote you didn't tell me."

"Oh," Oswald Snr laughed. "It is not everything that you put in letters."

After Los Puntos Estelares had played in Jamaica, Yunior had written home to let his parents know that he was coming to visit, but he didn't tell them how he suddenly had the means to pay for the trip. In return, he'd received his first letter from home for five years – a joint letter from his parents – full of excitement for his return, but also probing, trying to gauge what it was that was bringing him home as they'd had no notification from the government. His father asked if everything was alright at work; his mother asked if it was a family matter. Their euphemisms made him laugh out loud – he hadn't lost his job and he wasn't getting married, but it felt good that they were so concerned. He'd reflected on his parents' hands-off way of loving him while in transit in Madrid and then Cairo; it made him think of dew, how it could be counted on to settle on plants in the morning, although they spent most of their hours, the majority of their lives, without it.

Yunior noticed the flags draped around the city's ornamental trees and realised that he had arrived in time for the 6th of March celebrations. "Ah, Independence!"

"Yes, and our under-20 boys are playing in the '99 Africa Youth Championships. We are the hosts. I'll take you through Airport Residential so you can see how Accra has changed."

Yunior was silent as they cruised through Accra's wealthy suburbs, while his father pointed out new buildings and company offices sandwiched between old residences. Yunior recognised the older buildings – large homes put together according to the latest travels of their owners: Swedish-style, Dutch-style, Chinese-style… Of course, some of the homes, like many in Aguana, were remnants of colonial days and stood on stilts, like crabs startled by torchlight at night. A good number of them were still administered by the government. When he was a boy, his father had explained that the elevation of the houses was to protect the colonials from snakes and scorpions. The resulting spaces underneath the houses now harboured flashy cars, mainly silver and black. He wondered about the preponderance of those colours, but his eyes were drawn to the yellow-green leaves of mimosa trees and the loud brilliance of flame trees with huddles of scarlet flowers illuminating the roads like Japanese lanterns.

"You see here?" his father said as they emerged at the small roundabout that led to the Roman Ridge neighbourhood. "This is what I wanted to show you."

Yunior felt like he was in a foreign land. He recognised the area, but not its look. There was a multi-lane carriageway going one way, and, intersecting it was another that seemed to lead all the way to the coast.

"It's Kanda Overpass," his father said, his arm stretching out of the window to gesture. "It was finished some years ago. Remember how we used to have to struggle through the street market in Nima? This road goes right through, past Ring Road, all the way to Ridge."

"It's impressive," said Yunior, noting the omnipresence of street hawkers. No new road seemed to shift them or their wares: leather belts, air fresheners, groundnuts, sun-beaten puppies, frozen Fan yoghurt, framed portraits of Kwame Nkrumah, artistically arranged mountains of oranges and a range of car stickers vied for the attentions of drivers and passengers. It was as though a road was not a road, an intersection not an intersection without them. His mother was a more conventional trader, with her stall in the central market. He wondered now about the boys who were in Christian Methodist School with him, how they had fared while he'd been away. He was certain some of them would be very successful indeed, because trading of any kind could take you far in Ghana, if you were disciplined.

"How is Ma's stall? Is she doing well?"

"Ei, your mother? She bought me this car." His father chuckled as he manoeuvred the Beetle to the right lane. "She is doing very well. After you left, things were hard for a while, but when they got better, they got much better. You'll see the house."

The plot of the Osabutey home in the humbler section of Adabraka had always been large, but as they arrived, Yunior noticed that the house had expanded to fill more of the space. He was glad, though, to find that the trees had remained untouched, that the house was enmeshed in greenery. At the rear was a full-grown cassia tree that was three times the size it was when he left. The yellow of its shower of flowers reminded him of the sunflower on his roof. Musing on the origin of things, he wondered if his attachment to that lone flower was because of his memory of cassia flowers here in Accra.

His own grandmother – his father's mother – had been an uprooted sapling, a young trader from Mali who had fallen in love with a Ga man, Korkwei, becoming more wrapped in the traditions of his people than Korkwei himself, presiding over naming ceremonies and settling disputes in the market. Yunior wondered if the cassia tree, were it given time and space to speak, would say that its own roots were closer to the place he had just come from – across the Caribbean sea. Perhaps its leaves would glow with fascination at the notion that a tree from the Americas had become one of the ways a boy from Accra remembered home. Yunior was also trying to imagine what kind of bird could crack the hard shell of the cassia's dried fruit, swallow its seed, fly across oceans and, perched on the branch of another tree, excrete it into exiled existence. A few feet in front of the cassia, the mango tree was in bloom and the guava tree was heavy with fruit; on the ground, in the shade thrown by the mango and guava, close to the rear of the house, tiny pink explosions of flower revealed bɔkɔbɔkɔ in healthy abundance.

As he unfolded himself from the passenger seat of his father's new car, still daydreaming about trees, Yunior's mother flew across the yard from her lookout post – a stool on which she had been chewing tiger nuts – to embrace him. They held each other with the fervour of their lost years, their eyes closed against the weakening light as though trying to conjure their former selves.

"Atuu, atuu, atuu…" she repeated, running her hands along the back of his head and across his shoulders. "You've become a man," she said finally, holding his hands in hers as she stepped back to look at him.

Yunior noticed the flesh of her upper arms was looser, but her face seemed more relaxed than he remembered. She had tears in her eyes but she was smiling. He pulled her close again, unsure what to say. His throat was dry, his array of languages too blunt for all their fluency.

"It's what we prayed for," she said. "But you have been gone too long. Ah, ah, ah, come and look at me; Naa Okailey's son is now a man."

In the breeze-bred music of rustling leaves, Yunior smiled, finally finding his voice. "I bet you'll be asking me about your grandchildren next!"

"How did you know?" she laughed, squeezing his hands. "So?"

Yunior put his left arm around Naa Okailey, shepherding her towards his siblings who had held back on the verandah as though looking in on some private show. "Oooh, Ma!"

She ululated, clapping four times in quick succession. "My son is back." She gestured towards her other children. "Your brother is home. Baby Nii, go and get his bags from the car. Korkoi, come and hold him. Don't you remember him?"

Yunior had a room to himself. His sister, Jemima Korkoi (as he remembered she liked to introduce herself when she was little), down in Accra from Kumasi, where she was a student of medicine, was in the room next door, and Baby Nii, his youngest sibling, who had not stopped smiling since Yunior arrived, was in a room across the hall.

Their conversations were awkward to begin with. It was all inquisition and no exploration – like one's first steps in a forest. They danced around each other. He wanted to know his siblings as adults, what their ideas of the world were. Their questions for Yunior reached back in time to childhood and in distance to Fumaz; they wanted to remember when they had him with them, where they went, the games they played and they wanted to know what the country he lived in looked like, if Aguana was as beautiful as people said it was.

"It is and it isn't," Yunior said, stopping to start again in Ga when he realised that he had answered in Spanish. "It is like that and it is also not like that; for me, the most beautiful thing in Aguana is not the buildings (which everyone always talks about), not the beach – even though I love it – it's the peopleist approach, which we sort of have here too – even though it's not official."

Soon, they were chatting into the night every night. Their parents looked in on them, sprawled on Yunior's bed and shook their heads happily.

Now that they had settled back into the grip of their sibling bonds, speaking over each other and impatient to unravel all the mysteries of their separate lives, their mother delivered interventions in the form of snacks – groundnuts with roasted plantain, ginger-heavy sobolo, bofrot – and, during the day, reminded them when the Black Satellites, the national Under-20 football team, had a match.

Yunior was thrilled to discover his sister and brother alive with curiosity and ambition. Jemima wanted to specialise in orthopaedic surgery, mainly to help treat congenital disorders – the kind you saw on the streets in the poorer areas of Accra and around the country all the time. Baby Nii had just entered the University of Ghana at Legon to study French, Swahili and Arabic, and intended to serve in the diplomatic corps in the future. His current obsessions were Adinkra symbols, non-Italian operas and Ga naming ceremonies. They were clearly very comfortable with each other and Yunior felt lucky to be let into their circle so easily. He knew without a word being said that the money he had been sending to his parents would have been used to help cover the costs of his siblings' education. His parents were clearly content; they themselves needed no money from him – they wouldn't have needed it even if they'd had no money. Their contentment was the confluence of rivers, the unstoppable energy of nature's cycle of reunions – fruit and forest, seed and soil, rain and roots, moon and night, sun and day – three children all laughing in one room was enough for them.

For the first time in seven years, Yunior found himself thinking about the boy in the back of the laundry drawing clouds – Tomas and Flor's son, who had been separated from his parents when the secret police in Fumaz had picked them up. What had the boy missed being away from his parents? What joys had Flor and Tomas forfeited in their quest for wealth? Could he have done something to stop it happening? But he didn't do anything; he couldn't. He didn't know then which way their river was running, had no sense of which trees would wash their feet in that passage of water, what fruit would burst from flower and carry the juice of their dance – he didn't know what they were doing until it was too late. Yes, they loved their son and would have been thrilled to share many moments of laughter with him, but they also loved dancing and fine clothes. They also knew how ruthless Rosario could be – especially during *half-time*, specifically with those who profited from the food shortage while citizens were suffering. You love your country by suffering with everyone else; you honour the revolution, the blood of those who fought for liberation.

A question came to Yunior on the wind of the trees that had witnessed the last child he watched being taken away in Accra. He turned to his sister. "Korkoi, what happened to Teki? You know the girl whose mother left her by the…"

"Yes. She used to be here all the time, but she got an overseas athletics scholarship. She's in Canada now. Ma can tell you where her mum is, but I can give you her address."

"You mean his child?" Baby Nii asked, giggling.

Jemima joined in, breaking into laughter. "Yeah, you definitely have to go and see her mother!"

When his siblings spoke of love, Yunior paused, his mind alive with a cannonade of questions that seemed to have landed with him in this place of smiles, this place that held the germ of him like a thorn holds a scrap of skin and leaves a hidden scar. Tomas, Flor, Elena Burke, Marco, Omara, Manjate, Alberto Sanchez, Esperanza, George, the Gonzalez family – the names of his friends, musicians he loved and neighbours ran through his mind, but there were no clues in them. He realised that he had been holding part of himself in during his entire life in Fumaz; it was as though he still couldn't be sure of his place there. Or perhaps he had to return home to be sure of his family's love so that he could release that part of himself.

He had spent no time thinking of love and its possibilities in Fumaz. There was no one special. He smiled with the realisation, stunned by his own obliviousness, his head shaking.

Jemima said that for her there was someone, "But I wasn't sure what he wanted." She lifted herself onto her elbows so she was looking down at her brothers on Yunior's bed. "He kept making excuses when he promised to come and meet Ma. He didn't even meet Baby Nii!"

Baby Nii shrugged.

Yunior shook his head again, endorsing Jemima's hesitation.

After a silence in which they all seemed taken with musings as distant as the plains and crocodile-rich waters of Sakumo where legendary Ga Wulomei priests, elaborately coiffed and armed with powders and spells, roamed unchallenged right through the deepest incursions of British tricksters, soldiers, commissioners and looters, Yunior stood with sudden self-possession. "Would you like to meet my true love?"

He leaned to pick up the guitar resting against his suitcases. "This is her," he said. "Omarita." He gripped the guitar, sat on the bed and closed his eyes. Beginning with "El Manicero", he played through a medley of songs from son to Gyedu Blay Ambolley's "Akoko Ba", feeling himself travel through the music from Isla de la Innocencia to Bana and Aguana all the way back to Accra. He experienced all the emotions of his journey – his initial loneliness on Isla; his more settled transition to Bana, where he felt grounded, embedded; his work with the band and his experiences with the clandestine enforcers of Fumaz; his relocation to Aguana that was comfortable, but not resonant – a bit like his return to Accra. When he opened his eyes, his entire family was watching him, applauding.

"My son, I didn't know you could play like this," his mother said.

Yunior tapped the guitar. "This is how I made the money to fly for the visit."

"Can you play this?" His mother hummed a hesitant melody, her pitch just on the cusp of too high. "It's 'Daughters of Glorious Jesus'."

Yunior listened and played, until Naa Okailey was convinced that her son was actually a musician as well as an agricultural scientist. His father watched, silent, his chin cradled in his right hand, nodding all the while, until they both left the room.

With their parents gone, Yunior taught his siblings the basic steps of salsa and played for them, the guitar's hum floating through the mosquito meshes of open windows. Yunior's siblings shuffled their feet in the image of his example. Jemima was a natural, her movements easy as a cluster of cassia flowers swaying in Accra's spirited wind; she heard the music in her feet. Baby Nii approached the dance with infectious energy; it would take him a while to master its subtleties – but they had time.

When Yunior told Jemima that he'd hopefully visit for her graduation from medical school, he paused, then corrected himself. "I *will* be here for your graduation. Maybe I'll be back by then." After a few days at home, Yunior did not envisage his return with real conviction, but he felt that he had to speak of it. Having spent his footballing, musical, dating and baseball-playing adolescence – his fear, euphoria- and fire-filled formative years away from Ghana – he had stopped feeling like an oddity in Fumaz many years ago.

The Ghana Independence celebrations came: colour, scissor-cut costumes and dust-raising hordes consumed the streets with their movement. Parades and ceremonies, migrations to the beach, excursions to the hinterland by pilgrims who had forgotten, who could no longer conjure the foundation of the nation in its trees. In the red of the flag and the English of the anthem, they had lost the memory of Tohazie, a legend centuries before wooden, ocean-crossing ships had reached their country's shores. He, burdened with a dedication to shooting so true that distance didn't matter, had evolved into a warrior who could climb trees without using his hands. He unleashed arrows as he climbed, leaving his targets no respite, the curve of his bow as sure as the acacia sapling from which it was fashioned, his arrows as consistent as the weave of baobab root fibres that cradled them before their flight. Tohazie's heroism had underpinned the bravery and resilience of the nation's northern kingdoms.

It was always like this: a loud celebration of forgetting. It had been this way since Nkrumah's fall; since the military government that followed and the civilian one after, and the new military relay governments; since Yunior – as a boy – had endured one such parade in his school uniform under a sun as yellow as the ribbon that holds the black star in the nation's flag. He had marched the hot route without any reflection on the fact that the very backbone of Ga culture is a tree. What is a weku tso if not the tree that holds the family together, now morphed into the word that marks a neighbourhood – akutso? With the Gonja, is kingdom-founder Ndewura Jakpa's seat, Yagbon, not a tree? Does the title he inspired – Yagbonwura – not declare him a big tree? To see into the green past would be to see fallen Yagbonwuras carried in the carved core of a felled silk cotton tree to their burial site. To see into the green past would be to see the founding of the Asante kingdom based on the survival of a tree. To leave the green shoots of a nation's history in an invisible past is to march forward with no hope of growth. But there are trees along the parade route that have grown, that whisper their histories in the breeze while prison officers, police corps, army cadets, school children, uniformed nurses, customs officers and immigration officials march past to be inspected by president after president, whether bearded or clean-shaven.

They watched all this on TV, mother, father, brothers and sister huddled together on the terrazzo floor in front of the sofa as though it was the old home with no sofa. Yunior noted how the once thin Flight-Lieutenant Jerry John Rawlings he remembered from his youth was now a filled-out civilian president, though his voice carried the same energy and fervour. He felt that something had changed although the vessel remained the same. The route was unchanged, though the trees had grown thicker or been trimmed for convenience. He was home, but he was not. The flags waved their red, English-bred forgetfulness, their black star carrying brightness, their green – history gone invisible in a forest of new desires. And the drums played.

A day later, horns blared on the streets in the way only Accra could orchestrate. The Black Satellites had won the Africa Youth Championships, beating old foes, Nigeria, by a single goal. Women, men and children were out in the streets dancing. The flag of Ghana flew a million flights under a million stars. Yunior stood outside the gate of the Osabutey home, eating kelewele with Baby Nii and Jemima, who was soon to return to Kumasi. He had his arm around his sister, a flag dangling from his left hand, with breeze from trees that knew his odour keeping him cool. He had three weeks left in Accra, but he was already missing it; he was missing it because, watching the wonderful chaos outside, the energetic dancing, the tongue-in-cheek jama chants, the fantastical recounting of the action that led to the winning goal, he realised that he was observing like a tourist.

AGUANA

There is the odd night in Aguana when you can see a Cooper's hawk slide across the city's sky, its wingspan fully-extended, gliding on the hot air that the machinations of warm-blooded humans produce. It was on one such nights that Yunior saw his first sunset since arriving back home. He was on the roof, in the midst of his cuadrado verde, humming an indeterminate tune of loneliness, tapping on his guitar, Omarita, and silently thanking the gods for the random logic of nature that meant that while he was away, the crops he had on rotation were all hard-wearing, self-sufficient marvels. Yes, the lettuce had overgrown and sprouted shoots that would eventually yield seed, but the okra, red onions, frijoles negros and aubergines were thriving as though he had no part to play in their life cycle. He had stopped to put some structure to a tune in his head, hunching over the guitar to shape an E chord when a shadow fell over him. He lifted his head to see the Cooper's black head and off-white belly framed in the orange-purple of Aguana's dusk sky. He returned to the guitar more buoyant, and the song developed syncopations and layers like the crashing waters of the Malecón returning to remind the coast that their love could not be severed.

Lost in the song of his ruminations, Yunior took little notice of Aguana's sly dance to darkness, how the shadows of the boys playing by the sea slowly disappeared, couples fell into each other, and his lone sunflower became the brightest thing on his roof as the 29th of March leaned seductively into the 30th. He was simply a man with a song and his neighbour had to clap across the gap between their homes before he realised that his telephone was ringing.

He balanced his guitar against the ledge next to the sunflower and ran inside.

Marcos's voice was an animated storm in the melamine handset. "Have you been lounging in the depths of hell, brother? This is the sixth time I've called."

Yunior laughed. "Sorry, Marcos, I was far away…"

"A lot has changed since you went. Come and meet me for a cafecito – and you haven't seen the new house. You are like a relic!"

"¡Vale! Tonight? I can meet you at Calle San Martín."

"Oh, we've been getting lots of calls to sit in and jam since we came back. There's a son-casino fiesta in vieja on April first. Come, come to the casa…"

Without moving from his seat in the shadows, nursing a rum with a dash of roughly squeezed citrón, Yunior could tell that there was a crowd outside waiting to get into the club. Every time he lifted his head, a dozen new people were in motion in the central dance area. Others, having grown tired of public eyes, found corners in which to mould their contours to each other. Body parts clad in green, orange, purple, black, white, red, blue, magenta, yellow and darkening with sweat, moved with steady, assured rhythms, locking into frozen postures when the drums required it of them. And Marcos knew how to elicit sensual motion out of dancers; since taking a spot on drums – switching from bongos to his usual modern kit – the energy in the room had gone up perceptibly. Yunior nodded as the band segued into Moré's "Mucho Corazón", after a syncopated piano solo. Classic bailarines de son took to the floor, celebrating the fidelity of the rhythms to Fumaz's original heartbeat. Around them, younger dancers spun, gyrated and smiled as though they were feasting on the sun. Then Marcos caught Yunior's eyes and signalled him to join the band on stage. As he slipped Omarita out of its case, he heard the band transition into a contemporary arrangement of Jonny Pacheco. Marcos wanted him to sing.

Emelina was at the bar when the singer joined the band on stage. Looking out of the wide glass façade at the reflections of light off the Malecón, she hadn't seen him rise to join the band. Her mind was still in the house she had left. She had spent the evening sitting on the arm of her great-grandfather's chair as he sipped from a glass containing freshly squeezed lime and cane juice, now and then tapping her arm as though to remind himself that Emelina was actually there. All around them milled family and friends, people Emelina was connected to but had never met before. Music blared from speakers placed strategically around the old storehouse. A dance area, close to where the service counter would have been, played host to old friends, mothers and sons, cousins and old flames, dancing to tunes selected by a DJ tucked in the left corner of the room. Abuelo Ernesto had tried to connect her to as many of the gathering as possible, introducing her, with his broad smile, as the reincarnation of his grandmother, Emelina. They would speak to her for a few minutes, then drift off to get drinks, to dance, to eat.

She slipped out of the small wooden door built into the grand door of the storehouse, wrapping her arms around herself, cold in the sleeveless blue dress she wore as the breeze from the Malecón hit her. Reaching into the small handbag that hung from her shoulder, she took out a mint, popped it in her mouth and raised her face to the skies. Her stash of mints and Big Green chewing gum were all she kept in her bag, save for a pen and a small diary. She carried no make-up. Staring absent-mindedly at the stars, she wondered about her tata, Elián, so near yet so far from home, and tried to imagine the voyages of the Fumazero who braved the sea that separated their island from USAs, to head for the promise of the unknown. She turned as the door keened behind her.

Ernesto walked over with the dark shawl she had left draped behind the old man's chair. "I'm sorry there are no young people here. They probably stayed away to defy their parents. What young person wants to go to a 99th birthday party?" He chuckled.

Emelina shrugged.

"He's very happy you are here. We haven't seen him this happy for a while. Not since your grandfather left."

"Why did he leave, Abuelo Ernesto?"

"Call me Lito," Ernesto had reminded her, before sighing his response. "You'll have to ask him someday. I can say some things, but I don't want to sound prejudiced. You can never fully know a man's heart – and when he has a family, you can know it even less. As you can see, we are a wealthy family. Even with the struggles we are still wealthy. But we used to be much wealthier; many of the families with our kind of wealth left when some of the more progressive peopleist policies started to come in. I'm not saying that's why your grandfather left, but I can tell you why I stayed.

"When I was born, our mother fell ill. In those days, that's how they described post-natal depression; she couldn't stand my crying, she couldn't feed me. My father, Mr 99 over there –" he gestured in the direction of the closed door – "he gave me to his mother to look after. He had no choice; he had to work and he had to be available for my mother."

"So, I was raised by Mamá Emelina. My mother was better when I was almost two, but I was so attached to my grandmother that I stayed until I was nine. Your grandfather was born in the meantime, so he grew up on the estate – I'll have to take you next time – but I grew up in this house right here with Mamá Emelina. She is the one who told me most of the stories I've been telling you. She also told me about her father and her grandfather; they were all hard working-men who started with little. I grew up wanting to be like them; I was never afraid of starting again. That's why I stayed.

"Sabes, she also told me about the women in the family; they were strong-willed, like her. They made things happen. Emelina Soñada…" He turned to point at the name etched on the wall of the building. "It's no accident that this is called the Soñada building."

Ernesto took her hand. "And you know what she would do right now if she were you?"

Emelina grimaced, "Not really… Dance?"

"Maybe, but not here, Emelina." Her abuelo rubbed his hands together as though banishing cold and preparing for a feast all at once. "She would go out and explore. She would find a place in this beautiful city where there is live music, where there is sweat and loud laughter – laughter that can split coconuts – and then she would dance."

"But, I'm here for…"

He shook his head, lifting her hand to his cheek. Even in the dark, she noted how her palm was the same shade as his face.

"Mira. You are not just here for your great-grandfather; you are here to discover where you are from, the source of the fire in your corazon. Papa is happy you are here. You know that the cake will be cut at midnight and he will want you beside him for pictures to be taken, so if you are here ten minutes before, it's perfect. ¿Si?" He slipped some money into her hand before letting it go.

"Are you sure it's OK, Lito?"

"Ay, mi pequeña chica, just go! Get away from here. Find some young folk, have fun."

Emelina pulled her shawl tighter around her neck, skipped the few yards that separated the old storefront from the main road and turned to blow her abuelo a kiss.

He waved. "I would go towards the right if I were you. There's a son-casino fiesta just up the road. Very good band. Vamos. Baila."

She did one of the voltas her mother liked to practise in their living room, her hair a wild halo in the moonlight, and headed in the direction he'd advised.

The older man laughed. "Asi, like that! Don't forget, ten minutes to midnight; Papa loves his photographs."

When Emelina got to the front of the club and looked back up the road, he was still standing outside the old Soñada store with his arm raised. She waved and joined the queue.

Inside, she ordered a daiquiri, still high on Abuelo Ernesto's enthusiasm and the novelty of being able to consume alcohol outside her home. In USAs she only drank with her mother when she went home to visit. Alae would make a pitcher of daiquiri with extra lime and play some Alberto Sanchez on the stereo. Together, they would dance, daring each other into ever more dramatic postures, singing at the tops of their voices.

The band on stage played with the rootedness of Alberto Sanchez, but with extra zip, a kind of exuberance that was hard to trace but impossible to ignore. It was unlike anything she had heard before, but yet familiar – her mother would have loved to be in her place. Emelina held her glass to her face, enjoying its coolness, contemplating her conversations with Papa Diego and Abuelo Ernesto. She was a Santos because her tata, Elián, had dropped Soñada from his name on arrival in USAs. Once settled, the family had switched to the USAs naming system, where the last name on the father's passport becomes everyone's surname, so the name Santos stuck. But Emelina's father had insisted on Soñada being put on her birth certificate. After being in Fumaz, in Aguana, in the Soñada house for just three days, she thinks she understands.

In her reverie, Emelina's shoulders move to the cross rhythms of the drum and double bass. Near the stage, the singer rises, clutching his guitar and seeking a path to the front. A man in a tightfitting orange shirt approaches Emelina to dance and she says yes with a shimmy of her shoulder, draining her glass and leaving it at the bar. As they move towards the dance floor, his hand leading her by the waist, an energetic flourish on the bongos – a rhythm burning with the temptations of hell – draws in a steady double-pluck tempo from the bass, then a familiar riff from the guitar. She looks up at the stage as her partner spins her round; the singer has reached the band, adjusting the microphone stand as he strums.

Emelina thinks the riff is from Johnny Pacheco. She is proved right when the man, the angles of his dark face catching the light as he opens his mouth, sings "Trienta Kilos", the horns responding in staccato unison each time he sings the chorus. The singer's shirt is a patchwork pattern of greens and black, the kind of fabric that one finds in South Asia and Africa and he moves from side to side as he sings, strumming the guitar with genuine glee, as though it is impossible for him to sing without movement. The band segues into an up-tempo song that she does not recognise, but its rhythms are so compelling that Emelina finds herself dancing with the dramatic flourishes that she usually reserves for days off college, visiting home, carousing with her mother. After the chorus has danced around them once, she recognises its second coming and lets it find life in the vibrations of her singing voice. Her companion clearly knows the song and is happy to match her notes with flattened harmonies, accentuating his own dance steps to play in Emelina's drama. She hasn't fallen into a song like this since her early teens. She lives in a home

71

of nostalgia; she had forgotten the sweetness of novelty, the joy of shaping her tongue around a new song in the language of her mother. On stage, the singer oscillates his guitar in a pattern that mirrors the map-making loops of honey bees that have found nectar in a far flung patch of petals. His movement has purpose and joy; his voice is deep and expansive; there is something distant but reassuring in the timbre of its rise as he sings "Vivimos Juntos". As the band slows the tempo to a hypnotic Elena Burke arrangement, she disengages from her partner with a smile and wave and returns to the bar for another daiquiri.

Emelina leans back against the bar, still shimmying, watching the band communicate by a combination of hand signals, head nods and whispers as they work though their playlist. She doesn't realise that she is staring at the singer as she lets the music run through her. She reaches for a stick of Big Green. Her hand half inside her bag, she notices the thin brown leather strap of her watch and angles her arm to look at its judgemental face. It is fifteen minutes to midnight; the band is in the middle of "Quizas". She drops the wrapper for her gum, unties her shawl from her waist and bolts through the door.

Yunior first noticed the woman while they were playing "Vivimos Juntos". She was dancing with a muscular young man dressed like a bird of paradise flower, throwing some dramatic shapes, clearly lost in the music. Her dance steps seemed to owe their roots to the original bailarines de son, but there was something untutored about them, an innocence smouldering beneath the age-old movements. Her hair glowed even in the dim lights, a mass of regal curls set free. It was only when she walked away from her partner for the haunting "Que Sabes Tu" that he realised that he had been holding his breath. He didn't know what to call the feeling, but he knew that he wanted to speak to her. Her position at the bar became the point on his compass that he kept returning to and after a couple of excursions he was convinced that she was staring at him.

Without moving, she made it seem as though she was flying through the entire club. One hand on a glass that she held to the side of her face, the other hand occasionally engaged in the clicking of fingers, but otherwise moving in musical circles, like the coaxings of a dreaming conductor. Before long, he was singing directly to her, his guitar riffs instinctive as breathing, his voice coming from deeper within him.

At the start of the classic "Quizas", he watched as she drained her glass, then reached into her bag. Her pose had lost its calm imperviousness. He saw it before she dropped the paper from whatever she had retrieved and put in her mouth, but he could not leave the stage in the middle of a song. She wrapped her shawl around her shoulders as Yunior was singing the final chorus. By the time Marcos had led the band on a closing loop, she had slipped out of the door.

Yunior tried to dart through the crowd, but people stopped him to thank him for his singing, to congratulate him on the international exploits of Los Puntos Estelares, to ask which part of Fumaz he was from... He went to the bar anyway, his eyes darting around for evidence of the time she had spent there, his nose alert for her smell. As he prepared to run out after her, he spotted the piece of paper she had dropped and picked it up.

Outside, there was no sign of her. It was as though she had disappeared into the wind rising off the Malecón. He slowed his run, stopping under a street lamp. Yunior knew that there were only two possible explanations – one was that it was April 1st and the universe was playing a cruel trick on him, although the time for capers had passed close to twelve hours beforehand; the other was that she lived very close, in one of the proud old buildings along the edge of the sea. He peered at the paper in his hand, a wrapper for a kind of gum that came only from USAs, and sighed.

SUN COAST, USAS, 2002

The news came on the wind, carrying hints of red tobacco and tints of blue hills. Its voice carried the roughness of tree barks scarred by names engraved by doomed, sweat-soiled rebels to immortalise their more fragrant sweethearts. From the under-growth of Emelina's mother's village, it wound itself around history's leg so it would be dragged to the city her seven-year-old father left. In Aguana, it jumped onto the shoulders of a travelling hurricane, bent under the dreams of families who would cross the waters between home and exile. Many years of the World Meteorological Organization's odd customs mean that if the wind is given a female name, its casualties will be numerous, but this wind's news is for one.

In her office, Emelina Santos kept a small rubber plant by the window and a small flowering perennial on her desk. The local florist had told her both plants were from Fumaz. The window was open as she liked to feel a breeze behind her as she worked.

It was open on the day the errant leaves blew in. Their green-yellow exuberance reminded her of that last night in Fumaz, three years before, when, after her great-grandfather's cake was cut and pictures taken, a storm, which had held its breath all night, firmly announced itself. A sudden whiff of damp, a few playful spits of water that made you look up, a wind that told the trees which direction to lean in and there it was – monsoon in its enthusiasm but yet warm-hearted. She walked into the rain and let it wash her, her mind still occupied by the music she had danced to earlier.

Emelina smiled at the memory, returning to read the report in front of her.

She was interrupted by her assistant leaning over her desk.

"Excuse me, Emelina, there is someone in reception to see you. He says he's called Jorge. He works for your family." His last sentence was pitched with the music of a question, as though he couldn't believe that she came from a family that people worked for.

Emelina ignored his tone, simply gesturing for him to let Jorge come to her desk. She wondered why Tata would send his chauffeur to cross two state borders just to come and see her. Was Elián in the car himself? She dismissed the thought as soon as she had it; her grandfather rarely left his house now, he summoned whoever he wanted to see and expected them to turn up.

Jorge, who had loved to tease her since she was little, wasted no time with pleasantries. "Debes de venir conmigo, Meli. Ahora!" He walked round the table to embrace her.

"Is the old man alright?"

"He's fine. It's his father…"

"Wait here."

It was perhaps by the providence of yellow-green leaves that the day was almost over and Emelina's supervisor at Sun View Women's Resettlement Center was willing to let her go. But in the bucket seat of her tata's customised Jaguar XJS she reflected upon what she had been told. Diego Soñada Santos, matchmaker of rice and sugar, son of her namesake Emelina Soñada, midnight cake-cutter… her great-grandfather was no more. He had gone in the way only a Soñada could, preserving his myth, his aura of prescient serendipity. Thirteen days prior, he had written three letters to be opened on his death; one, he had given to Ernesto, the other two he had put in a package, sent up north to Jamaica, to be posted to the Sun Coast, USAs.

Abuelo Ernesto had called from Fumaz in the morning to ask if a package had arrived for Elián. When his brother confirmed this, he told him, "Our father just died. He was looking out towards the Malecón; he had been talking about you. Be well, brother."

"Brother…" It was all Elián could say before he broke down crying.

Ernesto knew that his brother wasn't crying just for his loss; he was crying for his own stubborn nature; he knew he could not let himself return to Fumaz for his own father's funeral. He would have to mourn from afar, simply because he had once shouted at the old man that he would never set foot on their godforsaken island again. Ernesto knew his brother had never learned to back down or apologise – not even death could win an argument with Elián.

As the dark blue car growled up the hill where her tata lived, Emelina spotted him standing at the main gate, waiting. She realised that the car would have been visible from the house. He must have been looking out for them.

He walked her up the flagstone walkway holding her elbow, past the contraband dark blue door, to the same open seating area he took her to before she left USAs for her visit to Fumaz. The plants in the pots had grown larger, so the tiles were now largely obscured by the arrowhead plant's now-split leaves and the various palms' elongated expressions, making the area look more green than ochre. In between, rubber plants and ficus peeked, with the odd burst of a Bird of Paradise in bloom.

Elián embraced her, holding on longer than she had ever known him to, then signalled for her to sit in the swinging seat. He walked across the room to a side table and picked up an envelope, ambling back to her with the slowing gait she had come to expect, his back straight, his head held a little higher than usual. He held the envelope out to her. "It seems…"

She heard the crack in his voice before the words came out, understanding in that instant why his head was held so high. Emelina put her arms around her grandfather and settled beside him in the seat. They swung in silence, gazing south towards the Caribbean Sea, where waves pitched and plunged as darkness bled into the sky.

Jorge came into the room and turned on the lamps, nodding as he walked backwards to the hallway.

Elián handed Emelina the envelope, finishing the sentence he had started. "It seems as if I'm always giving you messages from Fumaz." He rose and tapped her on the shoulder. "I'll ask Marta to get us some food."

The mention of food set Emelina's stomach rumbling, the same way the leaves in her office had set her thinking of Fumaz. She slid a finger along the frail edge of the envelope, easing it open with a sense of foreboding that made her shiver.

Diego Soñada Santos's handwriting was a shaky but elegant script with ebullient loops, his letter written in blue ink on pale cream paper. Emelina carefully opened the two sheets to read. His written Spanish, like his speech, was unfussy but amusing, and by the time she had read the opening pleasantries, she could hear his voice as though he were still in the ornate armchair where he'd sat for most of his birthday.

"I know your grandfather probably made you believe that I was half senile, but a man in love can never be senile and I have loved all my life. I began with the love of my mother – a wonderful woman – whose father built the house where you came to see me. You can't imagine how happy I was to see you, how incredible it was to see the daughter of someone I last saw as a boy coming back to walk, to eat, to sleep in the house where I grew up. Your father did well to name you after my mother – you look just like her. It's incredible. I know I told you many times while you were here.

"I loved your grandfather a little too much and in doing so, I lost him. He never lacked anything, never had to work, never had to apologise. We indulged him – Alba and I. That is no way to raise a child, I know that now, but he was the only one with us – Ernesto was with my mother in Aguana and we were on the farm. I'm just glad Alba didn't live long enough to see him leave Fumaz. It would have broken her heart.

"I need to tell you about our name, Emelina. You have probably wondered since your visit how come I took my mother's name, Soñada. Maybe you haven't wondered, but I want to tell you anyway. My great-grandfather wasn't named as other people are; he had just one name – Soñada – which he chose for himself. But because he laid the foundation for everything we have, my mother – your namesake – agreed with my father to switch their names as a tribute to the original, el grande Soñada. That's how I became Soñada Santos instead of Santos Soñada. Alba was a Fuego Marquez, so our boys became Soñada Fuego. Your grandfather decided to change back to Santos Fuego when he got to USAs, which is why you are a Santos. I am going to be a hopeful old man here, and ask that you consider adding Soñada to your names. It is not a demand, but it would make a dead man very happy. (Yes, I will be dead by the time you get this, and the idea is that you can't argue with me.)

"This brings me to the real reason for my letter to you. I want you to have a piece of what Soñada started with in Asadon. I actually wanted to leave you the small cabin that your grandfather was raised in. I built it with my own hands because I didn't want to live in the main house; it was too big for us. We were a young couple, we wanted to be close together. Anyway, that's what I wanted to leave for you, but your abuelo Ernesto has refused to inherit the rest of the land from me. He says his whole family are city-based now. So, mi hija, the entire estate is yours.

"It sounds like a lot, but the land produces little now. When we started using sugar on the land, it was like a miracle. For us, it was a political statement, but something happened to the rice; people couldn't get enough of it. Before long, our great leader, Guerrero Rosario himself, was being catered for exclusively with our rice. As his beard grew faster during that period, the myth of the rice also grew; we couldn't keep up with the demand, but each time we said we had run out, people would offer to pay double in advance for the next harvest. Even USAs government have someone here who buys for them in spite of the embargo. Soon our harvest was sold before we could ridge the land and irrigate it. We could have sold thirty years in advance – it was incredible! Your grandfather had left by then, but he still made his fortune from it; he became the main distributor in USAs and other foreign territories. Of course, you know Soñada Sun sells more outside Fumaz than inside – our people can't afford it.

"Ernesto, of course, realised the soil couldn't keep producing with all that sugar so he worked with some young scientists to develop a rice variety that gave a similar taste. For the last ten years, we've only produced a small quantity on the estate – we blend it with a fixed quantity we produce at other farms at our mill, which is also in the Western Provinces in Bana.

"I am saying all this to make you comfortable about accepting the land I am leaving you. It is more or less worthless as farming land, but I sensed that you love this country of ours even though you grew up away from it. I am giving you a piece of land that you can live on, something to give you a tangible link to your roots, a place to belong to.

"In a way, I am glad that Ernesto didn't want the land because this way I can give it to you whole. Every part of that land holds a memory; my great-grandfather pieced it together like a quilt from small plots and it remains a symbol of our family, a sign that disparate things can belong in one place. You may find some distant cousins on the surrounding land, but most of the Soñada are now city dwellers, like me. We have let the original families that worked for us continue to live in the quarters we built, but many of them work elsewhere. *They live without paying anything to me and I would like them to continue to live that way.*

"So, do not mourn me. Make the land of your fathers come alive again. I lived a full century, I lived simply and I was never unhappy for long. It doesn't take much; find something or someone to love. If you love sincerely, with all your heart, even pain is cushioned. Seek love, mi hija. I can't tell you how, but you'll know when it comes."

Yunior wiped the side of his guitar case with a small patchwork cloth he kept in his back pocket and leaned the instrument against the wall behind the stage. Since the first time he had accepted Marcos's invitation to sit in at the son-casino fiesta, the club, Hípica, had become a second home for both of them when they weren't hard at work or doing shows with Los Puntos Estelares. A few times a year the entire band played there.

He untied the bandana from his head and mopped his brow with it, then ambled to a seat close to the front of the stage, stopping to shake a few hands and accept friendly outbursts of chévere. Marcos was still on stage, leading the band in a rendition of Joe Arroyo's "La Rebelion" that had the crowd screaming their approval. Yunior caught the barman's eyes and signalled for a Balboa beer. He leaned back in the chair, not expecting the beer to come quickly as there were so many people in the club. There was a group of twenty in the middle of the dance floor who seemed to have come together from one of the provinces for a weekend in the big city. Clad primarily in shades of green, as if by mutual consent or in solidarity with the more verdant part of the country from which they had come, they appeared to be having a wonderful time. Every so often, they would form a circle and one of them would take centre stage, executing a signature move or giro that set the others cheering. It reminded Yunior of a celebration dance he had seen on television from Venezuela when

Hugo Chavez was re-elected as president. He had been in Nicaragua for the first time, playing two nights with Los Puntos Estelares to raise money for earthquake victims in Masaya, and was surprised at how night life in Managua seemed to have come to a standstill for the election results to be declared. The whole region seemed to have a vested interest.

Yunior felt a spot of cold on his right shoulder that seemed to be spreading. He looked up to find a bottle of Balboa beer held loosely against him by a hand with cerise-painted nails. He turned in his chair to see who owned the smooth, even-toned, dark hand and was stunned.

"It's already paid for," she said. "Remember me?"

It had been over seven years since he had seen her over the arrest of Flor and Tomas, but there was no mistaking the loose black curls that crept beyond her shoulders, or the assured posture. He took the beer and chuckled, gesturing for her to sit by him. "Are you following me again? I work for the government now, you know."

Loretta laughed, a sound as scattered as startled pigeons taking flight, settling herself close to him. "Yunior, you are such a cynic! No." She slapped his thigh. "I was working then, but I liked you – couldn't you tell?"

"You are very direct, you know?" Yunior raised an eyebrow.

"Why walk around the perimeter when I can go straight into the forest? I have to play games in my job; I don't like to do it in my life." She leaned sideways until Yunior could feel the rise and fall of her chest as she breathed, hear the creep of her hair as it swept across her shoulders and the rear of her fitted dress. "So, would you like to dance?"

This is how the story of Yunior and Loretta begins. Before long they are seen walking in the green and grey of the city; along flagstone avenues, by the low walls that separate human traffic from the hum and shuffle of the sea, and in shaded, cultivated squares where heliconia, torch ginger, hibiscus, marigolds and bougainvillea bloom. Sometimes, under the shifting blush of early evening skies, they dance intense bachata on Yunior's roof to an audience of spring onions, tomatoes, sweet potatoes, heart-shaped peppers and cabbages – or sit, staring up into stillness as he plucks at his guitar strings. Their heads are always close together; they are constantly in intense discussions, even as they stop to watch musicians coax melodies out of battle-scarred horns on street corners.

"All these people who leave, Loretta, how do you explain it?"

"People have their reasons; I can't tell you because I don't feel the same, but I don't judge them. It is not my place to judge. I have a job to serve the interests of the people and I do it." She turns to touch Yunior's face. "Why don't you leave?"

He is dumbstruck for a moment before he realises what has happened to him, how much like her he has become, and how easy it is to answer the question. He smiles. "I love this country."

"They are out, by the way." She flicks a strand of unruly curls behind her ear. "Last year."

When Yunior says nothing, she continues, "The son is about to go to university, Flor is teaching dressmaking. She was retrained in jail."

He picks a bit of fluff off the side of his blue trousers, then sighs, "I heard."

"Sabes," she says. "My parents met here in Vieja – my mother is from the Western Provinces, where you used to be; my father is from the East, he fought in the revolution. He was only 19 when they prevailed. He came to the city a couple of years later to study. They couldn't have lived here in the old days. They couldn't afford it. You know what happened when Rosario started to lower rents and convert rental contracts into sales contracts?"

"I've been told," Yunior nods.

"So, if some of the landlords chose to sell fast to grab large sums of money to buy property on the Sun Coast in USAs, I can't blame them. However, I can see... I have seen how the losses of each one of those people, those families, became the benefit of many. It's complex. Those of us who were poor can see the value of the revolution more clearly."

Loretta and Yunior walk on through days and weeks, music fading behind them, fingers intertwined, still in debate as they ascend the staircase of his apartment building, to the cuadrado verde where plants flourish under the sun's eye, where an olive eavesdrops to gossip later into the night winds. By the reflected light of a lone sunflower plant, they dance, igniting fires that only the sweat of naked flesh can extinguish.

In the morning, renewed by fresh mint tea – his with a touch of ginger, hers sweetened with three teaspoons of sugar – they lean over the balcony, watching abuelos and abuelas in the routine of their morning exercise, the blue of the sea behind the moving bodies and the orange glow of sunrise seeming to bestow those gathered with youth.

She points out the clarity of the sky to their left, how one can see as far as the old castle that used to be a holiday home for the dictator who ruled before the revolution. A place where there was a pond and feeding privileges for a band of flamingoes that became too lazy to stand on one foot as their heritage demanded because they knew that the water temperature would be regulated for them. An exhaustive range of beasts had lived on the grounds for entertaining the dictator – drunk monkeys from St Kitts, crocodiles, camels, solenodons, foxes, racoons, anteaters, an Indian elephant, royal pythons, grisons and wild cats. Particularly famous was a duo of tigers who were so readily fed giant sloths, deer and tortoises that they developed a disdain for any other flesh. When a unit of revolutionaries arrived to take control of the building, the caretaker – a recently retired member of the dictator's entourage of body-guards – set the tigers on them. The tigers, having smelled the sweat of the invading warriors, just slunk off, leaving Sergeant Carlos Ferreira Nevada pleading for mercy.

"Is it true that there are prisoners there?" Yunior asks. "Political prisoners."

Loretta pauses, as though weighing the value of her liveli-hood against the answer to the question. "The simple answer is yes, I guess." She shades her eyes from the rising sun and exhales. "This is one thing where I don't agree with Rosario. It's not the only thing, but when he speaks I see what drives him. He believes that all that we have achieved, all that we can achieve, can only happen if we do it together. So – this is my thinking – when people say things that will deviate opinion from the way he sees things, he feels the need to silence them, to put them away." She holds up her hands. "It's no excuse, but it's what I think. I believe people with vision, with an ideal view of how the world can be, can be blinded by that view – it can make them tyrants. I mean, none of this is by accident – these people exercising, the free universal education, your beautiful garden up here… it all needs planning…"

"But *half-time* still happened," Yunior says.

Loretta's arm drops from the ledge and she looks sideways at him. She sidles over to the makeshift bench beside the sunflower, where Yunior likes to play songs at night and drops onto it. The yellow head of the flower, now heavy with seed, leans towards her as if to conspire.

Yunior walks to her. "I'm sorry. I didn't mean…"

She raises her hand. "It's nothing. It's just that it's a question I struggle with myself. A lot of the party faithful lost trust in Rosario when that happened and I don't think he has got their trust back. In fact, only the beard kept him in power. Ex-Brigadier General Buendía's was only four inches shorter.

"He said he was preoccupied with the bigger problems – instability in Africa, here in the Caribbean, attempts by USAs-supported groups to unseat him, the earthquakes in Panama and Costa Rica... but people said, how can you say you are a visionary and be looking at Iraq and Angola and India and Kuwait and Sierra Leone and not see what it happening within your own borders, that people can't feed themselves. It was Rosario's worst moment, there is no doubt."

She shifts on the seat so Yunior can sit and she rubs his back. "But it's how I met you. Your work helped us save the situation. Now that you've told me your own story, I understand how you saw things differently."

Yunior smiles. "Maybe he didn't see because he was not hungry." He regrets saying it as soon as he has spoken, because he knows he is compromising her. Her job demands that she reports people who express thoughts like this. He hopes that he has been subtle enough for her to let it pass.

She holds his cheek with one hand and points at his forehead. "You! And you say I am direct? Yes, it is true, Rosario does not live an entirely humble life. Pleasure is a hard thing to resist – even for the most dedicated of idealists."

She places a hand on his chest and leans forward. "For example, it is now 7.30am on Saturday and you usually practise your guitar from 8.00am to 9:30am. You are a dedicated, principled musician with great fingers, but..." She moves the hand down Yunior's chest towards his navel. "If I say you will not practise today..." She grabs him by the waistband and drags him towards the door that leads inside.

It isn't until almost a year later that Loretta asks Yunior to help with a problem that Overseas Intelligence has raised. It appears that the new tactic of USAs is to use an initiative called the Global War on Dream States, a set of activities designed to reduce the consumption of dream-inducing narcotics (DINAs, pronounced 'dinners') in USAs, as a pretext to enter and destabilise territories where they do not find the governments sympathetic. Fumaz has been put on a list of emerging state-supported producers and exporters of DINAs and Rosario believes it is a step towards trying to justify an internationally-supported invasion of the island. Of course, it is people in USAs who are getting fat off the trade in DINAs, but that is not stopping their leaders from seeking the problem outside while settling old scores. Rosario wants to take no chances and a few tugs on his braided beard reveal the wisdom of approaching Yunior and the research unit to help counter the Dream States conspiracy.

Yunior frowns. "I don't see my role in this."

"No," Loretta insists. "There are small pockets in the Western Provinces where there is cultivation. We believe that groups from Honduras and Nicaragua have been coming in boats to help set up coca farms there – to diversify their growing locations, to avoid detection at home."

"But how can I help? I make farms more efficient; I thought you wanted to stop them from cultivating…"

"Yes, that's the genius of Rosario's idea. To make farms more efficient, you also control weeds, tengo razón? He wants you to consider the coca plants as weeds and develop ways to curb their growth. He says if we manage to do that, the global media will hail us and USAs will have no excuse to come here."

Yunior shakes his head, but he knows it makes perfect sense. He wonders for a moment if Loretta came to seek him out at Hípica precisely for this DINAs project, but it doesn't seem likely. No woman with the doubts that Loretta has expressed to him about the purity of the peopleist dream would invest twenty-two menstrual cycles in the solicitation of the services of a man whose dedication is already proven from past work for the revolution.

No – these no-backing-down discussions are theirs; these orange-purple sunsets and red-blue sunrises are theirs; these faded-brass-trumpet syncopated walks by the sea are theirs; these hastily water-coloured, fast-shifting evening tides stared at from an Aguana roof are theirs. Hers is his left eye that takes longer to open in the morning than the right, as though it is still running on Ghana's clock; hers is his bare back – dark, with the curve of a crescent moon – stiff in its protection of a melody coming from the guitar held against his thighs and belly; hers is his thick hair that arrests the light coming through the window and splits it into grades of luminescence. Their coupling has drawn its own energy, created its own power separate from the peopleist movement – a power with roots in bachata and the equator that draws such an elegant line miles beneath Fumaz.

Loretta did not come with him to attend his sister's graduation simply to see how the work of peopleist comrades was helping in the fields of medicine and marine biology (although she did see those things). She did not sit by his mother to learn how to cook Ghanaian dishes simply to outdo him in the kitchen or marvel at the fact that cebola is sabolai in Ga, that Ghanaians also cook malanga, make stews of the arrow leaves of its plant and call it amankani. It was not for agendas relating to the revolution that she took him to the sea-hemmed edge of the East, to meet her parents who had moved there to be teachers, or to the beautiful shores on which they dozed and dreamed and broke the burnished carapaces of lobsters to consume the flesh within. And the revolution was not present when they ran screaming along the beaches and got lost in caves hidden behind sea grape, dropseed, mahoe and rich green vines and found each other in caves damp with ocean spray and pungent with salt – or when, waist deep in the impossible blue of the Caribbean, their bodies stilled beneath the reddish eyes of a sleepy sun before erupting into ripples that would carry traces of their corporeal intoxication all the way to the shores of Columbia, Venezuela and Guyana. No – all that was theirs. His is the soft rise of her belly of kumquat freshness when she comes out of the shower, with down as fine as a kiwifruit's skin that tickles his nostrils; his, the quick éclat of her low heels as she smooths her dress over her buttocks and rushes down the stairs to work; his, the mischief in her eyes, the goose-pimpled anticipation of his naked skin when she places her hands on him.

But the revolution will not be derailed, will not be denied. Yunior sets to work on the DINAs project, working with biologists from the universidad in Aguana, travelling to the Western Provinces where experimental plots are cultivated under the watchful eyes of cadres.

Every known enemy of the Erythroxylaceae family of plants is recruited from field, laboratory, damp cave, forest, desert – even from the pampas on their neighbouring continent. Fungal samples come alone and with their substrates; moths come laden with eggs that have larval intentions; small rodents come in couples and as fiercely-shaded spinsters and bachelors; insects come scratching inaudible musics against the insides of the glass jars that have become their terrain. From this firmament of nemeses, some star candidates emerge: the *Aegoidus pacificus*, a beetle of glazed brilliance, the precise shade of brown of the shoes worn by the lead biologist at the universidad, Profesor Eduardo Blades. It has black highlights that give it a distinguished appearance and ridiculous-looking antennae reminiscent of unhusked corn glued head-to-foot in sequence. Then there is *Eloria noyesi*, moths so ghostly that they might be doubted to have been in the laboratory were their incorrigible offspring not all over the place, enjoying their short larva days, getting high on free coca leaves. And then specimens from two different divisions of the kingdom of fungi – the *Glomeromycota* and the *Ascomycota* – all with enough potential to increase the velocity of Profesor Blades's speech. It is not enough that these creatures and fungi spell pestilent ruin for coca plantations; they must be primed to be resistant to all pesticides in existence and likely to come into existence from the collective imagination of the DINAs barons and their pharmaceutical teams. So, Yunior and Profesor Blades and the team set to work isolating, substrate-testing, cross-breeding, environment-simulating and bombarding their laboratory specimens with chemicals in a way that would make the most hardened of criminals bloom with tears.

Yet love remains alive in the world, beyond beetles and fungi, beyond the revolution. Love is the barefoot couple, his dark blue trousers rolled halfway up his calves, her shorts bright as sunset, walking the patch of sand the tide has bequeathed along the length of the Malecón, arms interlocked in the misty air as though embracing their youth. Love is the music that snakes along the streets of the city to meet them as they emerge at the end of their walk, hands enlaced, his head resting on hers mimicking the angle of sleep. Love is the song, scream and shout of the house whose shadow cuts across their path as they walk through Vieja to the wedding cake flats of the newer part of the city.

Marcos has a new baby – a boy – with a scream more powerful than his body should produce, which he pits against his older sister's shouts as she runs around their home in baseball-truck-kitchen role play. Tied to his home in Vieja, Marcos sings to distract the baby, to disarm his wife, to divert his daughter. Sometimes, for drama, he lets loose on his bongos, his eyes closed, his hands remembering all the places where the leaf-spread palms have made music, the voices that rose with those songs. The house resonates with rhythm, casts far-reaching shadows as the sun sets.

Love is a child spinning round to a song she has known

since birth on Paseo del Leoncio, experimenting with new turns, pushing salsa and bolero into one, pulling bolero's three-four into salsa's rapid embrace, igniting applause from passers-by, fanning the fire of the musicians playing in a cluster with only the cajón player sitting.

Yunior is glad that Marcos has a new baby, so he doesn't have to be the one who makes the band take a break. With the extreme hours they spend on the DINAs project, mindful of the machinations of USAs and the threat to Fumaz's sovereignty, when Yunior has free time, all he wants to do is go to the pale yellow building on Calle 41 where his flat is, tend his garden, softly strum his guitar and fall into the arms of Loretta. It is the first time he has had both work and love to occupy him; he likes it, but it is all-consuming. Occasionally, they visit Marcos and his family – Yunior carrying Omarita with him – and they all luxuriate in their love of music.

In the end the fungi win. That is to say that the work of Yunior and Profesor Blades and their team produces a range of willing and hardy pests for the coca plant, but it is the fungi that excite el profesor most. Probably because there is academic benefit in their unveiling. There is a whole world of undiscovered, unnamed fungi, and identifying, describing and naming one leads to publications, lectures, global recognition. Yes, there is the moth and its larvae that evolve over their time in the laboratory into pesticide-resistant gluttons with appetites so thunderous that the aftershock is a reduction in the larval stage of their life cycle. Consuming 4.8 times their body weight of coca leaves a day, they hyperblaze into hard-nosed pupae in just ten days, cutting thirteen days off the life cycle of the moth – paradoxically making them even more efficient pests. Then there is the beetle, still burnished but now highly resistant to some of the most noxious chemicals known to men – dead or alive – and also fire resistant for up to three hundred and twenty seconds at eight hundred and ninety-three degrees Celsius, sure to be the pride of coleoptera globally. Its eggs, laid in the bark of the plant, evolve into stem-destroying larvae. But these fungi – and naturally they have been named patriotically, with the most destructive (and therefore the most important) named after Rosario, using his second apellido and the second most effective named after Profesor Blades – are something else. They will take on the DINAs world with guerrilla stealth – no one will know what happened.

But most importantly, they are named, documented and Profesor Eduardo Blades is already writing a paper: *Introduced Fungi as Selective Crop Control Agents with the Use of Systematics to Avoid Decimation of Region-specific Flora: a Study of Two New Fungal Species, P. australia and A. bladisi.* Next year he has a PhD student lined up to explore *Novel Techniques in the Selective Culture of Fungi for Agricultural Interventions.* For the first time in his professional life, he actually wants to leave the laboratory to witness the large scale implementation of the DINAs project. A man not given to displays of emotion, Profesor Blades has been dancing a great deal recently, showing a never-before-seen talent for rumba.

He is particularly excited about what he calls the semi-hypogeous *Paraglomus australia* which he playfully calls the spy fungus because it's not fully hypogeous; it peeks above the ground, clinging to the base of the host plant's stem but remaining invisible because of its mimic green colour. But place it under a microscope and you'll find it has filaments as radiant and ebullient as the graphics that radiate from these new computers when music plays or the screen has been idle. A vesicular arbuscular mycorrhizal fungus, it is unique because it is not symbiotic but parasitic.

Alternaria bladisi, on the other hand, is a fairly standard fungus, a relative of the species that affect the leaves of citrus plants, but it is curiously partial to calcium, which has high levels of incidence in coca leaves. It is a subtle but devastating pest, manifesting as an almost imperceptible coating of white, only becoming dark and visible when it is too late to save the leaves it has infected.

So, pests will ravage crops as the sea turns on the island and ravages its shores. After a bad storm, the defences protecting one side of the Camilo Torres Isthmus, which leads to the furthest end of the Eastern Provinces, breaks down. The government unit that conducts the repairs – and we can all attest to Guerrero Rosario's lack of involvement in the making of the decision – opts to shape the new defence wall according to the lines of Rosario's profile so that one part of the island looks like a mass coiled from the lengths of his legendary beard, and the other looks like the profusion of strong grey curls that still adorn his head at the age of 78. Our ruler, marketing guru turned guerrilla master, Guerrero Candia Rosario Austral hated it, but his love of the country meant that he could not justify extra expense to rectify this strengthening of his relationship with our green island. It was a battle he could not win. So, Fumaz becomes a living expression of one of life's many conundrums – in the abundance of love, hatred lives.

As the hurricane season comes in November, a boon for the flying spores of fungi, Yunior's work on the DINAs project slows down. However the winds bring wonderful news: Loretta is carrying within her a new citizen of the world – it has a heart, but not much else at present. There is reason to dance and sing. Los Puntos Estelares play at Hípica, the whole band together again, with a large crowd that sweats with relief that Hurricane Michelle only kissed the edge of the newly fortified Camilo Torres Isthmus, causing no damage. Our leader's profile remains strong.

The band's reunion is joyful. Esperanza promises to deliver Yunior and Loretta's baby herself when it's due; George signs on as her deputy by lifting one hand during a piano solo and winking; Manjate gives Yunior endless high fives, walking to the front of the stage in the middle of songs to bump him with his shoulder. Marcos can't stop smiling; after all these years, he still corners Yunior occasionally to say, "Hermano, you really saved me in those *half-time* years. You are my brother for life." Each time, Yunior smiles at Marcos's bent for exaggeration and slaps his friend's shoulder. Close to the end of the show, they send Yunior off stage and Esperanza drags her double bass to the microphone to sing a bachata interpretation of Roberto Cantoral's "Regálame Esta Noche" in a voice pitched as deep as their camaraderie.

Yunior holds Loretta, a smile spread across his face, matching the movements of her hips. "Así, am I moving inside you?" he whispers.

Loretta slaps his chest. "Ay, you are a rude man!" Still, she smiles. "Not yet; I think it's too early for movement."

They wave at the band, secure in the privacy of their embrace. This dance is theirs alone – it is a clinging red dress, it is a voice with a hint of jealousy, it is low heels that keep a beat but move silently; caves behind sea grape and mahoe, nights in the light of a lone sunflower, black curls that tumble to the shoulder, the burst of heat that greets a traveller arriving in Accra, battle-scarred horns on street corners, goose pimples after a shower, dark brown torsos rising out of blue waters, a dance in the place they first danced together. Outside, other lovers breathe the sea air and watch reflections of lit windows bob like buoys on the calm of waters that hold our island in place.

It is always the wind that disrupts us, is it not? It is the wind that tests the bend of our tenderest saplings, nipping at our leaves to see if they will snap. It is wind that reminds us that there is still chill on sunny days. On a great island like ours, sitting in the dark battle ground of the Caribbean Sea, we have known hurricanes as ancient as breath and older than the smoke of the distant Soufrière Hills; we have built sea defences because of the hurricanes. We have built and lost houses to the hurricanes, seen our crops and clothes fly away on the backs of hurricanes. But it is the winds that remind us that there are storms beyond hurricanes.

The storm season proves to be of great help to the DINAs project. Yunior and Profesor Blades are given national awards for their work. Their decision to use a range of pests is devastatingly effective. The DINAs barons spend all their resources trying to control the visible pests. After weeks of failed interventions with pesticides, they send out gangs of young children to collect brown-backed beetles and pale moths. At night, teenagers with torches seek to illuminate the moths, but the green fields become like carnival sites when the children tie strings to the bases of the beetles' wings and fly them like spinning miniature kites; and the teenagers go on their hands and knees below the height of the coca plants to form love connections. In the gaps that the anti-DINAs science has imposed on the growth of these breast-high plants, they tumble, giddy with new awakenings as the ghost moths form star-shaped patches of light above them, while beneath this firmament of flying stars, ephemeral as dust parcels, it is el profesor's invisible fungal warriors that emerge real kings of the spectacle. The DINAs barons know this when they wake up one morning to find their plants all bent, bowing in the same direction, as if in supplication to an unseen god, their leaves suddenly dark, undone by *Paraglomus australia* and *Alternaria bladisi*.

Yunior dreams of a girl, his own daughter, who will wear the smile of her mother and the burgundy and white of his own early, sunlit days on this island of ours. He will hold her the way his mother held him, bundled against the dusts of history's long march through the plains and marshlands of

West Africa, her sweat tinged with the salt of the Atlantic, her bounty of milky nourishment as inexhaustible as the Niger river's blinking slash and sashay from the Guinea highlands through Mali and Niger, brushing its blue-green skirt against Benin's soft skin before falling into the oil-laden deltas of Nigeria, an emulsion as true and rich as the milk Yunior himself suckled on.

He will tell her tales blessed with the same dewy weight of his father's whispers as he tapped against Yunior's bare back to accompany the musical names of past Ga kings, a parade of ages, from Ayi to Teiko to Amugi, red-headed to impossibly muscled, the tender-hearted and mean-spirited, Adama to Ofoli to Tackie. He will tell the legends of their hairstyles and brass-handled swords and unmatched prowess as dancers, the sea-parting ferocity of their war cries shouted from shore and farm, from the tops of the highest, strongest trees in the land, trees whose barks are still hardened with the entire histories of empires, their white splinters, their delicate meshes, their yellow falls and proud emergence into new nations – the call and response of it all, echoing his father's coos to his cries.

Yunior dreams his daughter will walk barefoot between aubergines and lettuce on his single-sunflower roof, will dance along the breaking strings of his guitar long before the whirlwind of the streets claims her loyalty, seduces her with the new syncopations of cajón, twisted flugelhorn and double bass. His daughter will belong to the land she is born on, never doubted, never questioned – unless she decides to travel. He prays that if she travels, the reasons be sweet rather than bitter. He prays she will not have the skin and ears of a boy he played baseball against once, whose epidermis and ear trumpet could pick up the breeze and whisper of a helicopter from miles away. He would drop to the floor, hands over his ears, his breathing making sandstorms from the dry earth beneath him, his entire being never learning to understand how he could walk away from an encounter with those spinning vessels when everyone else was dead, when everything was burned. No, he prays for his daughter to know the peace of nightfall under Aguana skies and – if it is a boy as Loretta wishes – the same for his son. A serenity that allows the heart to beat as steadily as the ocean's call and response.

Yunior has had his fill of ghostly moths and the nefarious appetites of their offspring – small worms that wriggle like riddles, getting fatter by the minute as they devour the green flesh of photosynthesis. Yes, this is the beauty of growth, of reproduction, that these nebulous white forms can consume so much of the wealth of green produced by the careful labour of the soil and its diggers, that they fatten themselves to the point of pregnancy and make cocoons of themselves until they rise as majestic moths that draw light and awe and the wrath of land owners. His mind is on the miracle that wakes up beside him in the middle of the night, uncomfortable because her body is changing. He watches her hips grow thick, her breasts sit in a heavier curve, her belly rising softly towards him. And he basks in the compliments she gets:

"But you are so slim for twelve weeks; you look wonderful!"

"Are you sure, Loretta? But you look more slender than the last time I saw you."

Then the compliments turn to frowns from abuelas who think she must not be eating right. What she needs is malanga for good carbohydrate, more frijoles for the iron, something salty if sickness is stopping her from eating. She needs to remember to drink plenty of water. Now, Loretta herself is feeling tired all the time; she thinks it's just her body adjusting; Yunior is fussing too much, she will be just fine. But he won't let it go, so she finds herself, her hands linked with Yunior's, sweat forming in a fine sheen from the heat they generate, in front of Esperanza's desk.

Esperanza walks back into the consulting room, her heels clicking like typewriter keys and settles her files on the edge of the desk. She nods at Yunior with a stiff motion, then turns to Loretta with a smile.

"Loretta, the baby is fine." She pauses and Yunior can tell from the way her lower lip is hemmed in by her teeth that she is uncomfortable. "The baby is fine, for now…"

Yunior feels Loretta's hand tightening around his, her nails digging as though there will be answers in his blood, but her professional training is immaculate, she shows no emotion to Esperanza.

"You say things are fine for now. Is something going to happen to the baby?"

Esperanza settles into her chair, pulling the files towards her. She could not move slower if she tried. When she looks up, her eyes are liquid. "Something is happening to you, Loretta."

Pancreatic cancer is a ghost moth; its cells have an appetite so ravenous it is hard to tell when they will consume the very life of their hosts. Loretta has been gliding through the streets of Aguana, footsteps like feathers, sweeping through alleyways, tickling the edges of sea barriers, startling leaning buildings into uprightness; eyes with the restlessness of peacock plumes, finding patterns where shadows try to obscure them, lifting veils, raising dust to dance as motes in public light, shaking foundations; a whisper here to right a slipping peopleist, a strong arm there to thwart a counter-revolutionary. But while she danced her peoplist dance, within her others twirled – identity-less masses. Who knows what garments these cells wear?

Once she knows, once she's cried, once she's accepted their diseased life-cycle as hers, she imagines them as caecilians with their personality-free colourfulness, their featureless heads that look like tails so you don't know if they are coming or going, their rainbow joylessness, the bright egg-laying, fully formed persistence of their survival – subterranean or leach-like – that leaves few imprints – their growth as exponential as a worm curved upwards against the bother of a stick, the heat-seeking undertone to their tyranny. And she imagines herself fighting back; generating sacks of defiance inside her that will swallow the malicious, naked brightness of these feasting fiends, dim their light, make them dance slowly to her tune, as in a dappled nightclub's muted illuminations.

In spite of the frown Esperanza wears when she examines her, the badly meshed pity in Marcos's new-daddy eyes when he visits, as the year turns, Loretta comes to believe she will beat the cancer – at least long enough for her to show her baby into the world, look into his eyes and see a new world being birthed in the bewilderment of his gaze.

"But shouldn't we speak about it, just in case?" Yunior asks.

Loretta shakes her head, her lips tight as a secret. "No. I will be here. I have the best care possible."

"What if…"

"Yunior, no one can plan for death anyway."

"That's true," mumbles Yunior without conviction.

Loretta pulls him close to her and tickles him, giggling. "Laugh for me, chico. Why are you so intent on being upset about something we can't control?"

A weak smile softens Yunior's face.

"That's better," she says. "Besides, I arrested you, remember? I'm bicho malo… You know the saying?"

"Bicho malo?" he frowns.

She is suddenly animated, rolling to sit on top of Yunior. "It's the opposite of 'the good die young'; bad people live longer – bicho malo nunca muere."

Yunior laughs and pulls her down to kiss her. "Eres preciosa, sabes?"

"I know," she laughs.

Her optimism makes her strong. When she convinces Yunior to accompany her back to the east, it is not only to tell her parents about her illness, but to harvest sea grape, to make its juice the cornerstone of her diet. She has been reading about natural cancer cures. She excises meats from her diet, even the chicken and pork she loves, replaces them with increased amounts of carrots, broccoli and cauliflower. No longer do they count stars at night from Yunior's cuadrado verde while sipping on rum; she plucks his aubergines from the plant, begs him to come home with squashes – yellow and green, walnuts and pineapples.

It is not long before her enthusiasm wraps Yunior in its embrace. From his childhood in Ghana he knows the role fruits, herbs and barks can play in healing; from his training in Fumaz, he is aware that certain plants have anti-carcinogenic properties. When Yunior coaxes Loretta to explore beyond the sanitised edges of Aguana and rediscover the north in nature, it is not to seek red-footed booby birds, black orchids, iguanas, frigates, cascabele flowers or Cooper hawks, it is because he knows that there are patches of macadamia nut plantations left over from pre-Rosario days. He adds turmeric to meals that are already fragrant with red onions and garlic. To replace the sugary pastries she once made up rhymes about, he makes her bean cakes from frijoles negros, adapting a recipe he had learned watching the vendor near the park where he played football in Accra as a boy.

Loretta gains weight. The curves that add ballast to her smile reappear on her face, the swell of her belly shows more clearly, she glows with the radiance of the beets and strawberries she devours in the middle of the day. Her walk regains its stealthy bounce, the swinging gait that Yunior loves.

One Saturday in early February they rise early. Yunior can tell by the news that George will try to call him later in the day, but he turns off the radio and its analysis of tensions in Sudan, snaps the top button of his jeans into place and helps Loretta with the clasp of her bead necklace. They are headed for Asadon, to the old Soñada Santos rice estate. Yunior has been reading about the benefits of the smooth, pebble-like fruit of the açaí palm and remembered that there was a row of them close to the rice fields where the heavily watered soils were perfect for the blossoming of the palm's miraculous purple fruits.

Although Yunior has never been there before, some of the workers, through conversations with neighbouring farmhands, recognise him from his role years before, one of them signalling the playing of a guitar to emphasise his point.

Yunior shakes his head. "Hoy no. The owner, is he here?"

An older man, Rafa, inclines his head and wrings dry palms.

"The manager," Loretta ventures hopefully.

This time, all the gathered workers look to the ground and cross themselves.

Rafa clears his throat. "The owner… he died last year. There is a new owner, but…" He adjusts the waist band of his trousers, a slightly worn affair in a dark shade of burgundy. "Can we help?"

Yunior points towards an area barely visible beyond the outline of the mahogany trees that lead up to the main house. "Some years ago I was driving by and noticed some açaí palms near the paddies. We wanted to get some of the fruit." He reaches for Loretta's hand as though it is a form of authority. "It should be in season now."

A shadow slides across Rafa's forehead as he turns. "The palms by the paddies? With the violet fruit? It's edible? ¡No sabía!" He walks in the direction of the paddies, followed by the other workers.

Loretta tugs at Yunior's hand and they follow too.

After walking in near total silence past the ornamental trees that lend the estate its heightened elegance, one of the workers, a man with a complexion reminiscent of dried corn husks, with a missing front tooth in his upper row, turns to say: "The new owner is a woman."

Rafa, at the head of the procession, nods. "She is related to our señor Diego..." He pauses to make the sign of a cross. "...but she is from USAs. She came for the funeral, but she says she needs time to think before she returns."

"Typical," Loretta mutters under her breath.

Yunior chuckles and squeezes her hand, glad to see her in the combative mode that has been missing in the weeks since Esperanza first discovered her illness.

The entire cluster of palms has borne fruit and the workers stare at the great height of the trees, nudging each other as though the plants are something new.

"I never realised they were so tall," says Rafa.

The only woman in the small group goes up to a tree and slaps the trunk. "I used to climb these when I was little, but I can't do it in a skirt. Not with you pícaros here!"

Yunior looks up at the bunches of fruit, ranged and even, like the pendants of a curious array of purple chandeliers, and knows exactly what to do. These are the coconut trees of his climbing childhood, the ones in his neighbour's yard in Accra, but with more pronounced ridges on the trunks and thus – in theory – easier to climb. He strips down to his underwear as Loretta gasps and then giggles with abandon. The workers begin to clap.

"Rafa," Yunior nods towards the older man. "¿Tienes un cuchillo?"

Rafa hands him a thin but sharp knife with a handle fashioned of strips of bark and cloth. Yunior tucks it into his waistband and shimmies up the nearest tree as though he never progressed beyond the nine-year-old boy who twisted coconuts off their stems for Mama Aba on Friday afternoons. He did this task simply to watch her conjure the sticky brown coconut sweets that she made by boiling shredded coconut flesh and its milky water with sugar until it caramelised. She would roll them into threads before they set, cut them into roughly even lengths and sell them in front of her Adabraka house – a seasonal but profitable enterprise that made his childhood dusks sweeter, but alive with threat. The sweets she gave him for his help were sought by every child that inhabited the distance between Mama Aba's and his home, so he learned to blend with shadows and flora, almost gliding from tree to bush to squatting position behind benches, walls and clusters of posturing teenagers. His friends must not see him in those moments after receiving his bounty of Anlo candy, for he would be compelled to share. In that soft cleft between the last light of day and the grip of night, there was no greater threat than the obligation to reduce his quota of those sweets that looked like petrified animal droppings but tasted like heaven...

There is a ripple of chatter, then the woman who slapped the açaí palm, who is rooted beside it as if the ghost of girl in her still wants to climb it, sends one of the boys off to get a large piece of cloth. The band of workers flit back and forth, anchored to the stretched fabric, revelling in the experience of catching the açaí fruit that Yunior cuts down in the nests of their makeshift safety net. They clearly have little work to do.

From his vantage point at the pinnacle of the third tree, Yunior sees the growing pile of fruit below and is glad that he borrowed Marcos's car rather than travel by one of the trucks that ply the route between the capital city and the Western provinces. The açaí fruit is not the only reason he borrowed the car; he wants to take Loretta a little further west to Bana to surprise her. Yunior is certain that in spite of her surveillance work she will have no idea what he has in store for her.

He studies her in miniature from above, looking alive again, in constant banter with the gathering of workers. She is a picture of health, a reflection of her miracle diet; she is ginger, she is saffron, she is cucumber, celery and parsley, she is almonds and poppy seeds, she is sea vegetables green and the bright burst of red chillies.

Surrounded by a profuse border of flowering oleander, frangipani, bougainvillea, heliconia and azoids, the house in Bana looks like it has always been there. Julio Gonzalez's humour is evident in the royal blue exterior walls that contrast sharply with the polished brown of the railings, window frames and doors. Yunior cranes his neck to the right to see if he can locate the old barn behind the new building.

"Who are we visiting, Yunior?" asks Loretta.

Tyres crunch on gravel as Yunior pulls up to the front of the house and alights to open Loretta's door. He smiles and embraces her, then lifts an arm to the sky. "Remember how I once told you that some of my happiest moments were on the small farm I used to run here in Bana?" He walks her to the bottom of the step where a burst of white frangipani has cast a shadow over the wood. "I wanted to share that with you…"

"This…" Loretta seems unsure what to say.

Yunior laughs. "You could not have known. No money has changed hands yet. Yes, this is for us."

"But how?"

"The Gonzalez are my familia. I had already rented the barn in the back and the land and they wanted to give it to me as a gift – with more land. But I wanted a house. So we had to make a plan to surprise you."

Loretta pushes Yunior's forehead back, then his chest. Then she stands with her hands on her hips, takes in the building and shakes her head, her green cotton dress catching a gust of wind, before she reaches out to embrace him. "Thank you." There are tears in her eyes. "It's beautiful."

Yunior wipes her tears, laughing. "I didn't mean to upset you. You are still good at your job!"

"¡Imbécil!"

"Now that you know, I can pay the poor family." Yunior holds her arm and pulls her towards the back of the building. "Come and see the barn – that's where I used to live."

As they turn the handle and the old wood door creaks inwards, there is a shout of "¡Ay! ¡Estás aquí!" and before they can blink, a radio is blaring music and out comes Julio Gonzalez and his family and the neighbours. It is a festival of hugs and stories of who, where and what. A plate of pasteles emerges and makes the rounds and Yunior whispers *surprise* to Loretta. When the roast pork comes out, Yunior notices that they have prepared thin, spiced slices of aubergine and grilled them for Loretta. His appreciation for the Gonzalez family multiplies as the day runs towards night and they all break into dance. He is holding Loretta and there is food and moonlight and bachata – and she looks as radiant as she has ever been and she refuses to sit down.

"You're not tired?" he asks.

"No," she smiles. "I'm perfect. This is perfect!"

Yunior sings Johnny Pacheco's "Acuyuyé" directly into her ears as they follow the rhythms of other songs. It is, indeed, a perfect day. He can't wait until the baby arrives. He holds Loretta closer and buries his face in the night of her fragrant hair.

They drive back to Aguana under the pitch black canopy of the forest-embedded roads of Bana and Asadon. There is a light shower, but it is cosy in the car and they sing all the way, laughing when Loretta starts to sing a Los Puntos song.

"I have something that would be perfect in that barn," Loretta says suddenly.

"Really?"

"Yes."

"Will you tell me?"

She holds a finger up to her lips and bursts out laughing.

Up in his flat, they fall asleep naked, but without the energy to make love.

Yunior wakes to an orange glow in the the open window and the sound of Loretta coughing. He rushes to the bathroom to find her hunched over the toilet. There is blood in the water at the bottom of the bowl. Yunior calls Esperanza. Esperanza rushes over to take Loretta to the hospital, but Loretta does not make it through another night. Yunior's perfect day has been the dawn before the time when darkness would break. Loretta's apparent improvement masked and simply preceded a rapid decline, an exponential decline. He cannot understand how it was that she began to look and feel better. Was it simply the power of her mind? Was it just three weeks of self-deception?

Yunior is unable to fathom how within a week of her reaching a weight close to normal, she has gone. Then, like a kick in the chest, he remembers that if she has gone his child has gone too – at fifteen weeks not even Esperanza can save the baby. His friends are all around him, but he can't see them. All voices become the sound of leaves in a city street. He does not recall leaving the hospital. He does not know when he uproots the sunflower plant on his roof. He does not know when he places it on his bed; why he stares at it until he falls asleep. Blinded by grief, Yunior is a ghost moth spinning unanchored in the relentless white light of Loretta's absence.

The girl approached her desk, bright streaks of light from the setting sun silhouetting her briefly into anonymity before the door closed. Emelina made the figure out as her eyes readjusted to the more muted illumination of her office. It was Isabella, her newest colleague – young but incredibly confident. She was already the person Emelina felt closest to at work.

Emelina shifted two case files from her corporate law class to the right, almost knocking down the pot carrying her Fumaz plant as she did so.

Isabella's eyes were drawn to the pot. "Lantana, right? I see them by the sides of the roads all the time. I never thought of putting some in a pot."

Emelina felt a wave of anger followed swiftly by resignation. Florists would say anything to sell a plant these days! She was surprised that no one in the office had pointed it out to her, but, perhaps, having seen how ecstatic she was to have it, they didn't want to see her disappointed. She made a mental note to check if the rubber plant on the windowsill was an actual Fumaz plant. Everything about her relationship with the island was uncertain and had been for a while.

After Papa Diego's funeral she had gone to the estate he had left her, seen the small home he had built with his hands, sturdy in the shadow of the grand mansion. At that moment, every instinct called that she should stay, though she saw traces of doubt in the eyes of the estate's workers, but mainly fascination at her clear family resemblance. She felt warmth in their polite distance – as though they wanted her to have the space to grieve. But she was about to start her second year of law school in USAs and she had a great job helping women in distress that was flexible around her studies. She had just convinced her supervisor at the centre to let her start a singing therapy group, after hours, to give the women – their *clients* as she was often reminded by the management – another means to express their struggles. Singing had always been a wonderful part of Emelina's bond with her mother. She often felt euphoric after they lost themselves in song and she was certain it would help the women she worked with.

Many of them were not simply leaving an abusive relationship or claiming what was their legal right, they were abandoning a position that – regardless of how uncomfortable – they had become adept at surviving. Their improved situation was still a displacement; they were moths out of a cocoon, blinded by light. And in two months, the singing therapy group had become so successful that to allow her to be in Fumaz for two weeks she had to ask a niece of one of the women, Isabella, a senior in the Vocal Arts degree programme at Sun Coast Central University, to fill in for her to lead the singing sessions.

It felt odd to Emelina to watch the group on her return from Fumaz – she felt connected, but distant. Isabella's unfussy manner of attending to each of the thirteen women in the group to improve their singing technique, even as they poured their hearts into the songs, had unveiled an extra layer of sensation for them. They heard their own voices rising with greater strength, with sweeter tones, more beautiful harmonies, and they seemed to enjoy a kind of ecstasy along with the usual release the session gave them. Beyond the laughter and circles of chatter that usually emerged after singing, they seemed now to be testing their voices, trying out vocal runs together without prompting, stunned at the sounds they were producing. They didn't just look revived, they glowed.

Emelina allowed Isabella to continue leading the sessions; it was an empowering gift for the women to improve their technical ability, something that she could not offer them, as an enthusiast who had simply imitated her mother while growing up with no clue how to teach. But it was also convenient; it allowed her more time for her studies. Besides, Isabella had been recommended to Emelina by her aunt, who was already part of the group – herself a survivor of abuse – and Isabella seemed to understand more intimately what the women were going through and the discretion required when interacting with them.

So, what was supposed to be a two-week cover, ran deep into September. Isabella said it was no trouble if Emelina still had work to catch up on; the evening sessions with the women didn't interfere with her studies. It ran through October, when a wave of freak storms left a scattering of north-west pointing trees fallen across Sun Coast, and delivered an assembly of new migrants needing orientation, housing and language support – increasing Emelina's workload. It dragged through November, the month of her abuelo Elian's birthday, when the old man, disconsolate because of his own stubborn refusal to return to Fumaz and mourn his father, kept summoning her. It was now December and, as it had become clear that Isabella was now the de facto leader of the women's singing therapy, it was time to formalise her employment. That was why the girl had come to the office.

Emelina had fallen into the habit of thinking of Isabella as a girl because that was how her aunt spoke about her – "She's a good girl, she can help". But, Isabella was a young woman of twenty-one, well-read and street wise – one who wouldn't have fallen for the florist's small deception.

Emelina wanted to say something about how she appreci-
ated Isabella's energy, wit and drive, but the speed of the
sentiment simply twisted her lips into a smile. "How are you?"
she said, motioning to the empty seat to the side of her desk.

"I'm good," said Isabella, elongating her O sounds as she
took in the surroundings. "Wow, you have a nice office. I can
see why you don't want to leave."

Emelina took a set of duplicate papers from a drawer to her
right and placed them in in front of Isabella. "This is the
contract. Read through it and sign both." She paused. "It's not
the office; you know I'm in school and the women…"

Isabella looked up, her palm spread across the second page
of the contract. "No. The women will be fine. That's one thing
I've learned; if you need to do something for you, you do it.
The people around you will adjust. If they don't they are using
you and that's not healthy."

"But I understand them better, I…"

"But nothing. Are you the only person in this centre who
is the daughter of a migrant? Are you the only one who speaks
Spanish? These ladies will be fine; look at what happened with
Piedra."

Emelina knew she had been driven by her own mother's
experience with abuse and life in a shelter, a part of her life she
didn't speak of often, but it haunted every song she sang and
tightened the circle of each swivel in her dances. But Isabella
was right; her desire to stay had nothing to do with the women.
The women were survivors and many of them were determined to make sure the rest of their lives were as rewarding
and fun-filled as possible. Piedra, for example, had been
abused by a USAs boyfriend who taunted her every time she
threatened to go to the authorities to report him. He was sure
that because she was illegal, a mojarra, she would never dare
to go through with it. She had found out about the Sun View
Women's Resettlement Center from a friend and arrived to

seek housing – a simple escape. Emelina had worked as a researcher with the legal team to resolve Piedra's immigration status, so she could bring charges against her boyfriend and Piedra had won a substantial settlement. Her first actions after the payment came were sensible – she bought a flat and a scooter. Then she went a little wild, seeking pleasure wherever there was light or sound. After one weekend away she acquired a new USAs boyfriend; he had hypnotic green eyes, but he wouldn't work, watched college sports all day and smoked with her when she returned from her cleaning jobs. Piedra tired of him after four months but he wouldn't budge from the couch.

She had asked Emelina, half-joking, "How do you remove a potato from the couch?"

"You cook it!" Emelina said, before adding, "Seriously, you have to tell him you don't want him any more."

"You think I haven't tried? He thinks everything is a joke."

Emelina shook her head. "Then you have to show him it's serious."

Piedra, it appeared, took Emelina's comment literally. She had heard from a friend that her ex-boyfriend had been seen lurking in spite of a restraining order. She didn't go to the police, instead, she acted extra affectionate around her green-eyed idler, taking him out to eat in glass-fronted local restaurants, kissing him every chance she got, purring like a cat in his lap and fixing his hair. It didn't take long for her plan to work. The violent ex went up to the flat when Piedra was at work and threatened Green Eyes. When Piedra got home, the poor boy had packed his things and was trembling by the door. The TV was off.

"You've been messing with some real nutcases, woman. Real nuts!" He fixed her with those limpid green eyes then shook his head. "I'm done, Pee. I don't need this drama… " and he shot out of the door.

Before he was out of sight, Piedra was on the phone, calling the police. By evening, one layabout was on a bus out of Sun Coast State and one violent ex was behind bars…

Remembering this saga, Emelina agreed, "Yes, Piedra is something. But it's more than that. Some of them are young."

"You mean some of them are stupid!" said Isabella. "You can't save them. Like Carla and Maria? Your being here didn't stop them getting high on their settlements, did it? Listen, Emelina, we are women too. You know sometimes we have to hurt a hundred times before we understand. We all do. Even my papa, macho as he acts, tells me how foolish he was to lose my mother. They will be fine. They will all be fine."

"And of course, I have law school…"

"So there are no law schools in Fumaz, where one of your cousins trained and is now working for the United Nations as an international human rights lawyer?"

"Well, it's December – nobody leaves family in December."

Isabella laughed. "I don't know what to say to you." She signed off the duplicate document with a flourish and pushed it back.

Six months later, they are having the same discussion. This time it is in a new bar along Collins Avenue; Emelina is trying the novelty of an avocado daiquiri, while Isabella orders a simple classic – gin, vermouth, green olives.

"You've got to stick with what you know sometimes," she says, scanning the décor suspiciously. "Some of these new places are too flash for their own good."

Emelina laughs. "And you tell me I'm cautious!"

"This has nothing to do with you not going to Fumaz. I'm just particular with drinks." Isabella shakes her head as they slip into a standing booth a few feet from the bar. "I really don't understand why you are still here. I'm confused. What's keeping you?"

"You have to admit, things have been busy at the centre… and I'm in a good place with Jonah."

"Uh uh – no! You are not going to bring Jonah into this. Jonah is not the guy. He's cute and everything, but he's certainly not the one who's going to stop you from moving anywhere. He would follow you like a lap dog and – come on! – you're on a girl's night out with me. We've been checking men out…"

Emelina stares into the opaque well of her cocktail. Her mother had asked her the same question just over a week ago. They had finished an indulgent dinner of grilled chicken with lemon-doused couscous and sides of steamed vegetables and frijoles negros con puerco – what her father had called hybrid Fumazero, complaining to his wife about replacing rice with North African stuff. In the playful banter that followed, Alae poked the small paunch of Juan's belly at least thirty times, until he yielded, protesting at the unfair use of tickling to win an argument. He had gathered the empty plates and planted a kiss on Alae's forehead before heading to the kitchen. Emelina and her mother knew he was going outside to smoke a cigar before joining them for a cup of sweet coffee.

Alae had moved into Juan's chair, so she was right next to Emelina. She took her daughter's hand, turning it over and placing hers over it as she used to do when Emelina was much younger. Emelina smiled, noting that now she could see the edges of her own palm framing her mother's dark hand.

Alae looked up, holding Emelina's eyes. "¿Qué te detiene, mija, qué te detiene?"

Emelina knew she could not avoid the question. When her mother addressed her in that Fumazero tone, it meant no escape, no excuses. Tears rolled down her face before she could think of anything to say. She didn't know what to say.

"Ay, ay, ay!" Her mother shifted the chair again and held Emelina's head to her shoulder. "Don't cry. You don't have to

say anything, you don't have to… I will tell you something."
She used her free hand to stroke Emelina's head.

"There are things that come, paths that open in life where
you can't turn away. Even if you want to. We all know how
much you love Fumaz. Even if we only felt it, we knew it after
your visit to see your great grandfather – you wouldn't stop
talking about it. Of course, we put the seed in you. Sometimes
I feel we birthed it into you. From your first cry you walked as
if you were born under the sun over there. I mean, look how
we dance here – you and I… And since you went to the burial,
there is only one place you have wanted to be – your whole
body, your entire being shows that a trigger has gone off in
you. Your abuelo, Elián, has seen it even if he hates it; your
father has seen it. You will go there, so why delay?"

Emelina moved her head slightly.

"¿Sabes? I told you how I left your abuela Susie's home but,
you know, I was never angry at her. I just felt sorry that she
couldn't see. I remember, even at the age of fourteen, from the
first time she brought that Vincente home, that she would do
anything for him. Something came on in her eyes, when he
was around; her body seemed softer, her words floated out of
her. So when she spent a year thinking of whether to come to
USAs, I had already prepared myself to leave Fumaz; I knew
she would leave, I just had to wait for her to realise. I walked
the land differently, I planted things to grow in my absence, I
stored sand in jars to travel with – even the chickens we killed,
I killed them tenderly…"

Emelina giggled against her will, sniffing against her mother's wet blouse.

"So, you don't have to answer, but promise me you'll think
about it. Think about why you are passing your days in USAs
in a trance when you could be alive where you want to be…"

Emelina raises her eyes to meet Isabella's gaze, taking a long swallow of her daiquiri, savouring the sour bite of lime that undercut the avocado's smoothness, catching the pale rum's fire in the back of her throat. She puts the glass down. "I think I'm scared."

Her finger traces random patterns in the condensation on the outside of her glass. She feels lighter for having spoken these words – not enough to float, but as though she has thrown off some wet clothes. She realises that is what she was afraid to tell her mother. Alae had been through so much, but she was never hesitant; when something needed doing, she got up, tied her hair in that severe knot that Emelina has learned to love, and did it. How could she – a girl raised not to be afraid, with all the love and support possible, with the best education available – tell her mother that she was afraid, that she felt inadequate. She hadn't even admitted it to herself until that moment.

"Aren't you going to laugh at me," she challenges Isabella.

Isabella reaches out and taps Emelina's hand. "You don't laugh when someone opens their heart to you." She smiles. "At least, we know it's not Jonah – thank God!"

Emelina laughs.

"But why?" Isabella asks.

"I don't know exactly. I think when I went to the estate, I realised that it wasn't just a piece of land; it has a history – and it's a business. I was there for the burial, but I don't remember much of the burial – just a lot of cousins and aunties and uncles, everyone dressed in white and emerald as the old man had requested – but I remember the estate clearly. I can still see the light flooding into the corridors of the main house, the tidiness of the grounds, the particular hues of green that every plant carried. I had never realised that green was so varied, so vast.

"But you know what I remember most? The look that the workers had when my abuelito told them that I had inherited the estate. What I saw was not just people learning of a new owner. I saw families who had been on the estate for generations and they were looking at me with something close to adoration, like I was an anointed person – some kind of saviour. Imagine never having run any kind of organisation before and you arrive in a place where a group of highly skilled people embrace you as leader without question. There are women and men and children staring at you and they see someone who is going to make sure that they are OK."

Isabella shrugs. "You look after women and children here…"

"This is different, you know. So many people – whole families. And what do I really know?" Emelina sighs. "I just feel that if I stay here, my abuelo Ernesto will make sure everything is fine, but the moment I arrive… Well, if I'm there, I… I don't know!"

"You'll never know if you don't go."

Emelina is silent again, her mind filling with images from Fumaz, the tree-lined drive into the estate, the sound of music drifting up to the balcony in Aguana, the Malecón gleaming in the dark though a glass façade.

"It's not fair on your abuelo either. At least go and speak to him; it might help you make a decision."

Emelina nods. "You're right." She raises her glass again, but towards Isabella for a toast. "You are one mean little girl, you know? Here's to wise friends."

"I am not little, OK?" Isabella laughs as she lifts her glass to meet Emelina's. "Just make sure you go."

"You know it's my mother's birthday at the end of this month, right? So I can't go until July."

Isabella reaches across the booth to slap Emelina's shoulder. "Coño! You're impossible. Just promise you'll go, OK?"

"Yeah, I promise." Emelina makes a face and drains her cocktail, turning to look outside through the glass. A streak of red, like the rear light of a departing scooter, catches her eye and she follows its gradual contraction to nothing, her gaze tuned to its intangible distance beyond the glass. She doesn't notice her own reflection staring right back at her, all the mysteries of the world of drinks gleaming behind it.

It's the sense of time that goes first. When a body is mourning, watching clocks, sunsets, recording births and deaths, becomes a kind of erasure of self. That's why on this island of ours we say that we have a long history but a short memory. Most of us only remember Rosario. The years before, with the Spanish and the USAs Capitalites and the rebels, just sit in the background unexplained, like the weight humans put on between the ages of thirty and forty, that just goes and sits on the body, obliterating its own history, its own causes and origins.

So, it is Esperanza, with Loretta's medical records, who gets a message to her parents who travel west to Aguana to bury their daughter and the baby that proved to be a granddaughter who never knew the texture of light. Yunior is present in some ways not others. Whatever the trigger, his tongue still delivers the right language, the correct tone in response when he is spoken to. He is leaner, visibly so – his trousers hang from his waist as if by magic, the fabric billowing around the thin stalks he stands on. Less air is displaced from his mattress when he settles into bed, curls his body to find comfort, as he grasps the stem of the drying sunflower plant he uprooted in the fog of Loretta's death, now a staff to support him as he limps back into the place where only he can go – the space of shared memory. Except there is no-one else there, no way of checking facts. Still, there is enough to leave grains of sweet in the bitter. He is holding onto something that is fading, not faded.

The sheets are unchanged, the dust motes carry figments of her skin; her smell lingers enough to tease.

In Yunior's mind's eye every limb of Loretta's, every expression, is still vivid and can be conjured. There are dawns when he slips from sweaty dream to damp-sheet reality before his brain registers the what, why and when of his loss, when his body, taut from the seduction of its unused virility continues to writhe on the mattress, his face inhaling what's left of what he loved in the pillow, his mouth speaking to her absent responses as his muscles pulse slowly back to normal. He feels no shame in his release. He is grateful that he has enough of her left to lose control over, until the rising sun illuminates the now papery form of the sunflower. The tears come when they want, unbidden, like his spilt seed.

Yunior is present, but he is just a shadow of his full self. Some days he plucks seeds from the sunflower's belly one by one, counts in Ga and chews them.

He protests when Loretta's parents, Andrés and Lena, insist on taking him with them back to the East, to their little village near San Alegria, but he doesn't resist. Marcos has packed a bag for him. Esperanza hands them vitamin supplements they are to make Yunior take. It is this quiet efficiency of friendship that has kept him tied to the world. He has spent so much time in bed that he flinches when touched, his skin sore from the weight it has borne.

When Andrés walked him to the room, Yunior wasn't certain what he was supposed to be looking at. He had been at the house for five weeks and his routine was well-defined: he woke up and walked down to the beach, took off his chancletas and let the sand ease beneath his feet as he headed towards the rock coves where sea birds gathered.

He would sit on a black rock worn smooth by waves and wanderers and stare out to sea. This was not Accra. There were no canoes that appeared on the horizon and slowly gained definition as their home-painted hulls of blue, black, white, red and yellow got closer and closer until you could see their slogans play hide and seek with the slosh and slap of waves: *Give my enemies long life so they can see my success. A good name is better than riches.* There were no men to pull in nets here, none of the chaos and clamour, but the sea air, the gentle sprays, their calling card of salt on the skin, grounded him. He sat on the rock until the noise and light grew bold enough to move him along, until the birds became quarrelsome, and the sun's rays burned his neck.

Back at the house, he'd have a breakfast of stewed lentils, a boiled egg and mango, sometimes with a slice of home-baked bread. Andrés and Lena's cooking was flavourful but free of salt and low on starch, a regime for ageing constitutions. Andrés cooked fish for lunch, grilling his catch just outside the porch where Yunior sat after breakfast, doodling and humming obscure tunes. He missed his guitar. His friends had packed him off as baggage, a thing unwilling to live. He could not blame them for sending him on his way with the bare essentials. He had shown no inclination to do anything for weeks before Andrés and Lena decided to bring him here. He had certainly not wanted to touch the guitar with which he had serenaded his dead lover when they sat on his roof dreaming of a future that was now a vanished wisp of cloud. However, after the third week with Loretta's parents, he felt a yearning to do something with his hands, find a physical outlet for the feelings he could not articulate.

He joined Lena in her garden, finding comfort in the contact with soil. Occasionally, she would say something unrelated to the plants, clearly not expecting an answer: "Nobody wants to bury their own child." Then she would return to seeding sweet potatoes. She was a careful gardener, cultivating in neat rows and clearly marked sections; there was a lot of land, but she kept it with the care and attention of a windowsill gardener. Yunior had once complimented her gardening when he visited them with Loretta, and Lena had beamed all day, giving him extra helpings of spinach with the grouper Andrés had cooked. Her smile still remained, but it looked like it needed effort to keep its ends up. Even Andrés's cooking routine, formerly punctuated with jokes, reminisces and laughter, was reduced now to the crackle and spit of fire and fat.

Junior had been expecting Andrés to arrive with fish and seasonings when he got the tap on his shoulder.

"Es la vez justa," Andrés said, signalling for Yunior to follow him.

They walked down the main corridor of the house to the rarely used back door. It wasn't locked and it didn't seem like it had ever been. On the other side of it, across a patch of hardy grass, was a small outhouse. It was squat, but wide and had two green doors, one, to the left, narrow and tall and the other, slightly to the right of centre of the building, was a full arm-span across, with a wooden bar that ran parallel to the ground, acting as a barricade. Andrés strode across, lifted the bar out of its rests and pulled the door back.

There was a black rectangle painted on the wall closest to the door and a few bits of spent chalk, like discarded gravel on the floor beside it. The rest of the walls were unpainted but clean. Several books lay on their sides on a low shelf at the far wall, beside a sturdy home-made desk and chair, onto which light from the only window streamed. Right in the middle of the room there seemed to be a larger desk covered in blue cloth.

Still doubtful about what he was supposed to be looking at, Yunior took it all in, staring up at cobwebs that clung to the exposed beams holding up the roof.

"¡Allá!" said Andrés.

Yunior's eyes followed the path that the old man's arm traced to the large desk in the middle of the room, noticing for the first time a power cable snaking across the floor from behind the door to the desk, where it disappeared under the dust-dulled cloth. He also noted the echo that persisted after Andrés spoke, how it hung in the air even as he moved.

Yunior lifted the cloth carefully. He saw two sturdy legs and a high backboard, like the kind of desk that you store things in, but as he removed the cloth completely, he saw, between the second pair of legs, a set of foot pedals and understood that this was some kind of organ.

"Being a freedom fighter isn't easy," said Andrés. "In your own country? Killing some of your own people? Está loco! But at least you have the courtesy to feel for everyone you kill – I feel it still today. The Capitalites don't. Children died because they took extra profit rather than build hospitals, but they don't even consider it. You don't have to pull a trigger or stab someone to be a killer.

"People weren't the only casualties of the revolution." The old man ran his hand over the closed organ. "Many things like this were thrown out, hidden in cellars. When we drove into Aguana, saw the clubs that people used to go to... the owners, the ones who fled, had dismantled musical equipment, sometimes smashed guitars and sliced the membranes on drums, just so the band members, the poor working men who had kept their clients entertained all those years, wouldn't have instruments to play in their absence. The sidewalks were littered with old clothes, one-armed dolls, pig's guts for stringing tennis racquets, curiosities like mounted buffalo heads, drum pedals and endless bits of paper. Who knows what secrets were on those papers?

"Once we knew we were in control, we tried to salvage what we could of the debris. I found a child's piano, a Schoenhut. Nice brown wood, lovely varnish – a little chipped on some edges. The legs were gone, but the keys played just fine. I don't know why I kept it, but I did. Later, after she was born..."

Andrés's indrawn breath echoed over the exhalation that followed. The thin white vest he wore made him seem particularly vulnerable. Yunior placed a hand on the older man's shoulder, steadying both of them.

"When she was older. I took it out and polished it. She used to sit on my lap and play. I never replaced the legs – I would put it on the table."

"Loretta played piano?" Yunior couldn't believe that she had managed to keep something like that from him.

"She didn't play after she was nine. She didn't like to talk about it. But she was very good until an accident... Very good. She was playing with some friends after school. I am not sure you can call it an accident, really... You know we lived in Aguana?"

Yunior nodded.

"They were playing on the pavement when a man from

USSRs walked past. He didn't say anything; he just walked over them. He stepped on Lolo's right hand and broke three fingers. When she screamed, he looked back and yelled something at them. They could tell from the sound of the language he was from USSRs, but they didn't know what he said. So she couldn't move her fingers properly for months. When she could…"

Yunior heard the rebound of the sob before he registered that the old man was crying. He put an arm around Andrés and led him back to the house. They headed for the porch, where Lena was sitting, rubbing her foot absent-mindedly. She looked up and waved Yunior away, standing up to wrap her arms around Andrés.

It was the echo that drew Yunior back. The soft reverberation that tells you something is living, moving; there are particles carrying your message – even if the destination is the source. It was the echo that told Yunior that he was being selfish, that he might have lost his love, but he was living with a wonderful couple who had lost the one thing they had lived for. He still had music, he still had Los Puntos. It wasn't fair for him to load his misery onto them. But he wanted to be selfish a little longer; he had lost a daughter too. If he couldn't say it out loud to them, he would say it to himself.

He returned to the room, to the organ, because there were walls there that would listen to him when he said: *I have no idea what to do now. I changed an imagining of my life that was fluid and built all my dreams on love. How do I start again now that the love is gone?* He went back to the room because the walls couldn't judge him like people would. They would reaffirm him with a sound both alien and familiar, his own voice returning from the hard edge of the walls, with no self pity.

It was the echo that drew Yunior back, but it was the note that made him stay. He ran his hand over the box of the organ and tested the wooden foot pedals. He felt resistance. The low sound that emerged surprised him and he noted its source – a box speaker that sat beside the organ. Andrés had clearly turned the organ on already. Yunior smiled in spite of himself, making a mental note to thank the old man. Strolling into the light, he took the chair behind the desk against the far wall and carried it to the organ. He lifted the sculpted cover, marking its weight, the mild chipping where the felt-fabric rest of the keyboard's frame met its protector, and folded it back on its brass hinges. There were three levels of keyboard, like a mini flight of stairs, the first two bearing the familiar two-three banks of black keys interspersed with white keys – except with twelve inversely coloured keys to the left. On the ridge from the first level to the second, on a gleaming backdrop of black, was a word that made him smile. It was the family name of his cousins in Accra: Hammond. He hadn't seen anything like the third level up – a row of protruding bars with brown, black and white handles at the end.

Breaking the dark solidity of the organ was the white corner of a piece of paper. Yunior reached into the thin haven between the screwed-on bar that held the music stand, and the main housing of the keyboard, and pulled. It was a folded sheet and it bore his name in a scrawl he recognised. His heart stalled, like a nocturnal creature caught under a bright spot-light.

Yunior, mi amor, feliz cumpleaños. Remember how you said I carry so many secrets from my work that you are not sure if I will ever completely open up to you? Well, I have bought you this because it is both history and future; it is my confession and my promise. I love you so much that I don't know how to tell you; if I keep anything from you, let it only ever be this one thing, the expression of love, but know it – I love you.

I didn't know how to commemorate your 33rd birthday until we went to Accra and I saw you drumming with your brother and sister. You had told me that you didn't play any music before you learned to play guitar on Isla, and when I asked you later you said that drumming was so normal in your home that you never considered it an instrument. I realised then what I had to get you and how it connected us and how it would be the best way for me to share my last secret with you. People sometimes forget that the keyboard is a percussion instrument – even I do. When I saw you that day, with your feet tapping as you drummed, your sister and brother calling and echoing as you made up those djama chants, even adding my name and my shoe size to the story, I knew that I had to get you a Hammond organ. An organ because both feet and hands are used and I know you like challenges. I want to say something naughty about how you like to use your body, but my mother has a healthy habit of reading my notes (¡basta Mai!)… I will tell you tonight.

When I was little, Pai told me stories of musical instruments being thrown out, hidden and discarded after the Rosario revolution and I never forgot. So when I got this idea into my head that you could play and – I think – will enjoy playing an organ, I started asking around. I found it in Santiago de León, which used to be a weekend getaway for USAs businessmen. It was in the basement of a club that still has signs in English and is now a dance school. In Vieja, I found the pedals. As for the speaker, it is built entirely by Pai – I was stunned when he said he could, but then children forget what their parents can do. I confess my guilt. He is, after all, a trained electrical engineer and he practically built this house by hand. Anyway, that's who you have to thank – también for cleaning the keyboard and repairing some faulty circuits. Complex things.

The reason I never forgot the revolution stories is that Pai got me a small piano when I was little. A sturdy brown thing with no legs – it might still be somewhere because Mai never throws anything away! I used to sit on Pai's lap to play it and later I played piano in school. So, that's my confession; I play music too. Well, I played – and that leads me to the second part of my sharing. I haven't played for years because of an incident from my youth. It is also the incident that indirectly led to my career. I must have been eight or nine years old. We played on the side of the road a lot then – marbles, noughts and crosses, draughts, that kind of thing. One day a very large man just walked through our game, trampling us; I got the worst injury because he stepped on my hand and three fingers were broken. When I screamed, he just turned around, insulted us and kept going. No adult or authority was there to help us and it made me think that there needed to be more people helping to protect us Fumazero when things like that happen. Also, I knew the man was from a Peopleist country so I realised that just because people come from a Peopleist country doesn't mean that they live by Peopleist ideals – some people will only live by those ideals if they feel like they are being watched. So I joined the police force first, then when I was asked to join the special unit, it made perfect sense to me. And I can never regret it, even though we have spoken about things that I don't find ideal. I can't regret it because in February 1992 it led me to a young man I could never forget, a man that is now the father of the child inside me.

So, Yunior, my Kole, that's it. What connects us is music, too – we both had secret instruments, both instruments were percussion. I have no more secrets from you. We are completely in synch now; I belong to you, you have a home in me. I want to tell you again, because I can never tell you enough, I love you with all my heart. This may surprise you, but I love you more than this land of ours… so wherever you are is my home. Now, I have seen the way you are transported when you play music, I hope that this organ will help to add substance to those journeys. Feliz cumpleaños. 33 is a wonderful number; it makes me think of old records spinning… I look forward to watching you teach our children to play, like my father taught me (even though he knew very little). If they get half as much joy from those moments as I got, perhaps they will have the courage to find and follow the lure of music to its very end.

Yunior stared at the note, then held it to his chest, eyes closed.

The light from the high window played on his lids, making his existence a red haze. He sat motionless, barely breathing, until the first tears pushed past his clamped lids, his body shaking as short breaths escaped him. Her forthright speech, the tap-tap-tap rhythm of her walk, her head thrown back in laughter, the baiting light in the depths of her eyes. She was everywhere and he couldn't breathe, she was everywhere and his tears had no dam.

He folded the letter and put it back in its hiding place beneath the music stand, his hand shaking like a plucked string. He couldn't breathe, but he hadn't felt so alive since the day Loretta died. He held his shaking left hand over the keyboard and let it fall to rest on the first level of keys. When his breath and body had steadied, he played a single note, a low F, an octave and a half below middle C. Its sound expanded outwards, clear and captivating, struck the walls and returned, overlapping with its progenitor to develop a richer tone, like a mother and a son singing in harmony, the child impatient, the mother assured. Yunior closed his eyes as the sound bounced around the room, embracing him in its incessant chant. Then he lifted his finger off the key, waiting until he could no longer trace any strains of the note. He opened his eyes and pulled one of the bars on the third level out, a brown bar close to the middle, and played the same note again. The note bloomed with an extra layer of harmony, not unlike his mother's trilling when she didn't know the words to a song at a funeral. When he let the sound come to rest, he pushed the bar back in and pulled out the third white bar along from the brown one he had just replaced. Yunior played the F note again. A controlled shriek welded itself to the sound – wild, but in complete harmony as it rose into the light-charged air of the outhouse.

He remained in the outhouse for hours, playing note after note, pulling the levers and listening for the shifts in sound and mood, marking how like a human wail the organ could sound – from the agony of grieving siblings keening in a huddle, to the contented hum of a new grandfather rocking his daughter's baby to sleep. Yunior simply played; he made no attempt to shape any song, any melody; he just lent his ears to the vocabulary of the keys, rejoicing in sound. He played like a child, a broken-hearted child trying to forget why he feels the itch of tears in the depths of his eyes. His fingers, accustomed to the severity of strings, found a subtle comfort in the smoothness of the Hammond's keys – a soft landing, a second home. The unique twists that each pulled bar added to the notes he played became companions, their peculiar overtones increasingly recognisable as the light in the room faded.

In the swelling darkness, he let his hands play over the full range of keys and experimented with the bass pedals at his feet. From the seeds of his experiments, reeds and leafy shoots of music rose in the shadows, enveloping Yunior in their juxta-positions. The echoes off the walls became the murmurings of a forest – the rustle of rodents in undergrowth, the lingering fragrance of fallen flowers, the cries of crickets and cicadas. He was lost in a new world of sound. There was a note for the kisses he could no longer have, a shriek for the empty arms of a bereft father, a harmony for the lost sag on Loretta's side of the bed – and the sound only stopped when he lifted his fingers, only subsided when he was satisfied with how much he had pummelled the walls with his grief.

Without the intervention of Andrés, who returned to the outhouse to coax him away to eat, Yunior might have stayed all night, playing in the dark, building a new home in the soundscapes of the Hammond. He left the outhouse knowing that he would be right back. He left thinking he had a sense of what peace might feel like.

Emelina kicked her legs up, still cocooned in the shell of her purple sleeping bag, and let them fall slowly back down, bracing her hands behind her head. She felt the muscles in her stomach stretch and her entire body strained as her feet returned to the cradle they had left in the old mattress. She repeated the action, feeling the effort more with each repetition. She had planned to go for a jog, but she felt it would be too soon to be seen running around the estate when she had not yet met all the workers. It had been less than 24 hours – there weren't even sheets on the bed she had slept in! Wriggling out of the sleeping bag, she left it in a soft heap near the foot of the bed and stood up.

The old cabin was a stunning piece of architecture: pragmatic, sensitive to its surroundings, aesthetically pleasing. Built into the rise of a small hill, it looked smaller on the outside than it was inside, its wood floor level where the hill had been dug to make way for the rocks that formed the cabin's foundation. She imagined Papa Diego breaking boulders from the eastern end of the estate, where they huddled among tangled roots of ceiba and acacia, and hauling the resulting rocks here. How satisfying it must have been to finally walk the floor, the wood resonant underfoot, what was once bare earth now cradle to a kitchen, a bathroom and a bedroom that ran, through double doors, to a porch the size of the walled part of the cabin. The porch was clearly the heart of the building, the rooms just required for the realities of life.

Leaning on the east-facing railing outside, experiencing her first sunrise in Asadon, Emelina understood why it had been built this way.

The sky still purpled with night, the early sun peeked through the thick bases of the roots of trees lined up like troops on the eastern front, rising to filter patterns of light onto the land spread before her. This was Soñada's legacy: acres and acres of rolling, verdant land, still bordered by the trees that made up the forest that was here before the Spaniards and Portuguese. These were the trees her mother dreamed of, the trees that nurtured rebels and soothed their loves with the texture of their barks – trees with messages in their sap. There were no blue hills in Asadon, but Emelina dreamed of her mother visiting, returning to the land that dwells in your heart forever.

She looked to the left, where she could just make out the hedge that bordered the main house. Like her great grandfather before her, she had found it too large and was drawn to the cabin, which was away from the entrance to the estate, behind the main house and had its porch and steps turned away from the cultivated world towards nature. Arriving from Aguana the afternoon before, she had found the main house daunting, a reminder of the enormity of her responsibility. In spite of Abuelo Ernesto's reassurances, she needed time to ease into her role.

"You have time," he had said, smiling, holding her hand as though he could not believe that she had actually returned. "The place is efficient. The families know exactly what to do to keep everything going. They just need to know that the estate is in family hands and they will keep at it. You don't even have to stay all the time…"

"But I want to, Lito," she insisted. "I want to understand the place. I want to feel my place in it."

"You will, mi pequeña…"

Emelina shook her head. "I know what you mean, but I don't want to be here just leading a life of leisure. I want to help. If I stay on the estate, I want it to be alive, like it used to be."

"All I'm saying is that it took you over a year to get here. A little extra time won't hurt. It takes time to understand that not everything happens as expected here." Ernesto opened his arms to embrace her. "Hey, you should visit that club again. This time I can go with you, see if this island of ours still has real dancers!"

Looking over the estate, Emelina wished for his calm assurance, his sense of fun, his easy relationship with the families on the land.

Emelina felt the sun's rays getting stronger, warming the side of her face. She turned back to the horizon of trees to witness the stunning orange paint of the sun's rise, the night's residue now banished, the sky becoming clear and blue. Shielding her eyes, she walked to one of the two wooden chairs facing each other in the centre of the porch as though in some interrupted conversation. She sat in the one facing almost east, slightly away from the direct attentions of the sun, placed her feet on the other and closed her eyes. Now that she had spent the night and really seen the estate, the nature of her family's peculiar relationship with the land was becoming clearer.

There was still plenty of fallow land; a capitalite farmer would say that the land was underutilised. While the property was called the Soñada Santos Rice Estate, there was only a small amount of land suitable for rice – in the gentle valleys at the front of the estate, on either side of the tree-lined drive to the main house. However, because Papa Diego had told her that Soñada had pieced together the estate, a sort of moving map of hasty deals, mirroring rebellions, instability and infidelity on the island, she understood why the terrain was so varied.

The family had lost much of the flat lands to the first Capitalite-backed government when the road was built. Farms on the other side of the road produced far more rice; it was only Papa Diego's accidental genius that made the Soñada Santos Rice Estate the most successful in Fumaz.

Emelina leaned back further in the seat, placing her right forearm over her forehead. She was going to speak to Rafa, the workers' representative, later in the morning. She had been dreading the moment, unsure what she could say to a man who had worked here for so long, but she had just thought of something. She felt that her idea was important and sensible and it came from a statement Rafa had himself made when she asked about work on the estate.

"The money is good; we don't have to worry about that. We get paid from the head office in Aguana and they send trucks to collect the rice when we harvest," he said. "But we don't produce so much anymore. When you work on a farm it feels good to produce a lot, ya sabes?"

"I see," said Emelina. "Ernesto told me that the rice harvest has been reducing."

"Señora," Rafa stopped with her bags at the steps to the cabin. "It is more than a reduction. The last two years, we only got a crop because we saved seeds from the harvest before. None of the new rice seeds grew – only some of the ones we had kept. The soil is no longer any good."

"So how many tonnes did you harvest?"

The old man chuckled. "Ask your abuelo later."

He climbed the steps ahead of her and placed her bags at the double doors, pointing at a key in the lock before lifting his hat with a smile. "Duerma bien, dueña."

"Good night, Rafa."

It was clear to Emelina that the rice paddies were barely producing anything. Her great grandfather's letter had alluded to it, Abuelo Ernesto's 'es complicado' when she called him last night admitted it and Rafa's diplomatic responses confirmed it.

Since they were producing most of the rice in Bana anyway, there was little point in keeping up the illusion of rice production here at Asadon. Yes, she resolved, she would tell Rafa that she considered it best that they stop rice production at this estate and ask him to tell the families. Later she would meet them and consult on what other crops they could cultivate on the rest of the land.

Emelina stood up, headed for the bathroom. She felt good about her first full day at Asadon, her imagination dizzy with the country air, its tincture of secrets, histories and the long-suffering sap of its green bosom. She looked forward to her meeting with Rafa. The estate would have a whole new life and, of course, Soñada Sun, the family's rice brand, would remain safe, its supply covered by production at the newer farms in Bana.

Yunior slipped back into his flat in Aguana as stealthily as our great leader's beard hangs; everybody knew but nobody broached the subject. Like the beard, no one dared approach the object, but he was watched. Marcos, who had been dutifully squeezing time from the infant-filled chaos of his own home to visit weekly and clean the place, simply stopped going. Manjate, who kept the cuadrade verde watered and healthy, kept his distance. Both men realised in hindsight that they had found solace in their moments alone in their friend's flat. Esperanza, who knew beforehand that Yunior was returning, stocked his cupboard with some essentials and didn't visit. They were all unsure how to reset the connection that they had with him. There was no manual for the turn his life had taken and he did not seem in a hurry to reach out for their support either. He appeared rootless yet a certain calm emanated from him.

When he didn't return to work and, three weeks later, left for Ghana, they went right back to keeping his flat going. Who knows what it is that drives a grieving person back to their original source of comfort, back to the seed of themselves? When a tree is cut, it doesn't fall upwards, it falls to its roots.

It was when they went back to filling the space he had left behind that Manjate noticed that Yunior had planted a new sunflower to replace the one he uprooted right after Loretta's death.

"There's life in him yet," Manjate told the band at rehearsals. "I'm sure he has just gone to inform his family of the loss. On the continent we do not send bad news without a mouth to speak. He will be OK. He just needs time."

Marcos flexed his arms upwards, holding his drumsticks in a loose grip. "I hope not too much time," he said. "I miss him."

"I do too," said Esperanza. "And the band is not the same without him, especially now that George has gone to Sudan for a while. We are three of five."

She turned to the yellow-shirted man sitting behind the keyboard for the rehearsal. "Sorry, José," she said. "You always play well, but there is nothing like the original band playing together."

"True, José," Marcos added. "But the man we are talking about, Yunior, is no threat to your place in the band. He writes and sings and plays guitar."

"He's a complete dreamer," said Manjate. "Calls his guitar Omarita."

The three friends laughed as one and José joined in. Then Marcos counted off with his sticks and the rehearsal began. They were soon in harmony, with Esperanza singing in place of Yunior and Manjate backing.

But they had planted in José the seed of his disposability and it grew as relentlessly as a sunflower watered by an Angolan on a rooftop where lovers embraced and guitar chords slipped into song. He played better and audiences could feel it. The notes blossomed beneath his fingers, their sound as clear as the ocean's undulating hiss and roar by the Malecón at night, suffused with a yearning as tangible as a held breath.

The band was busy, and had been since Marcos had been able to reduce the time he spent looking after his now-walking son and his daughter of boundless energy. They played at least one night a week, often two and sometimes three. And every night, the flying ants of José's plea for belonging swarmed listeners and dancers and bit them with pentatonic clarity. The fever of the dancers' intensity heightened, and listeners went home sick with yearning, reached across the barren spaces in their beds to find solace in whatever their hands fell upon.

Yunior returned to Aguana in the fullness of June to find his sunflower in unmitigated bloom. Having had to relive his sorrow through his mother's grief at the loss of a grandchild, his spirits were in need of the fast-growing plant's yellow resilience. He inhaled its seedy heart, his shadow merging with the sunflower's own projected question mark. The olive tree remained as stoic an observer as ever, only a mild swishing of its leaves betraying its presence, its weakness for breeze, its ties to the life of the island.

The rest of his cuadrado had prospered too: aubergines swollen with healthy pigment, herbs punching the air in pungent ecstasy; peppers bright in their rudest colours. He resolved to call on his friends and thank them for their silent care after a quick trip to see Lena and Andrés and the Hammond B3. He had no space for the organ in the city, but anytime he wanted to feel connected to Loretta, he would go and visit, play the keys and spend some time with Lena and Andrés. This time, he had gifts from his mother to deliver to them; next time he would go as the son they had told him he was to them.

Ambling inside, he picked up Omarita, sat on his bed and strummed an Alberto Sanchez classic; his new musical secret, a portable Korg, remained stashed under his bed, still as an untapped emotion.

It was Manjate who spotted him leaning like a fruit-laden papaya tree in the doorway of Gente, where they were rehearsing, and shouted, "Yunior!"

After Flor and Tomas had been imprisoned for the counter revolutionary selling of vegetables, Gente had become a centre for teaching dance to escuela básica and secundaria students after school, but it was free on Wednesdays, Saturdays and Sundays, the doors unlocked and swinging occasionally in the wind like a waiting embrace. Many bands had responded to its call and Los Puntos Estelares, who used it on Wednesdays and Sundays, were no different.

They stopped mid-song and converged on Yunior, José lagging behind, his hand leading as he waited for Marcos, Esperanza and Manjate to finish hugging their friend.

Marcos slapped the guitar case on Yunior's back. "Ah, you brought Omarita. Good!"

Yunior took José's outstretched hand. "Soy Yunior. ¿Qué tal?"

"Es un placer conocerte finalmente. Yo soy José."

"José is filling in for George," explained Esperanza. "George has been gone longer than he said."

"You're good," said Yunior, letting go of José's hand. I've been listening to you. I like the way you play on the Pacheco…"

"What do you mean by you've *been* listening?" Esperanza cut in.

Yunior laughed. "Let's just say that this is not the first time I've watched you rehearse. I learned a few things from Loretta, sabes?"

He had said Loretta's name without thinking. A result, you could say, of thinking about her every day for four months, or of railing against her to the walls of a one-eyed outhouse during daily hours-long sessions with an organ that she left him in place of herself, or because he had been talking to himself so much that he had lost the skill of withholding the seeds of thought that others should not hear.

Esperanza smiled, but did not respond, planting an adolescent silence in the room.

"So are you here to join us?" asked Marcos.

"It's OK to speak about Loretta," said Yunior. "She's never

coming back; I know that. But I don't want to forget her either – or my daughter. I came to thank you all for looking after my place while I was away. I hoped to play with you, but I'm not going to stay if you are just going to dance around me."

Silence returned to the room, more defiant than before. The light from the doorway framed the band in stillness, the ocean's ancient air the only thing moving.

Then Esperanza opened her arms and said, "Ven!" Yunior smiled and walked into the embrace, tears welling in his eyes. Manjate and Marcos added their arms to the huddle and even pulled José in.

Four songs later, when they took a break, the sun's light less charged as it filtered in, Marcos sat next to Yunior on a low bench. "Hermano, it's like you never stopped playing. That was great! Your runs are more complex."

"Thanks. I was nervous, but it's good to be back." Yunior fondled the wet neck of his Balboa beer bottle. There was so much more he wanted to say. He had lost so much, but he was grateful too. The money they had made together as a band meant that he didn't have financial worries; he was lucky to have this group that he had known for years to embrace him after his time away; it was magical that they had music as a shared language, that he could just fall back in rhythm with them. However, his flat was still empty, his heart still ached and he knew none of his Los Puntos Estelares family could fully understand what he was going through – how sometimes he needed to tune out of their joy, how he had to suppress occasional urges to scream. The words jostled for order in his mind, making him close his eyes momentarily. He placed the bottle on the floor and stood up.

"I'm not going back to work," he announced, the sun fading behind him.

The phone call from Abuelo Ernesto was short, matter of fact and over before a conversation could start. Emelina frowned, letting her eyes scan beyond the double doors of the cabin to the horizon, where the sun had risen over the barrier of silhouetted trees. It was the period just before high noon, when even ghosts looked for shade to shelter in. The estate families had left the vegetable patches they kept to find pools of cool air within their homes. Like all our Fumazero, they snacked or sang or schemed or slept, snug in solitude or shared history.

Emelina was surprised by the call because Abuelo Ernesto had visited her just two days earlier, his eyes glinting through every exchange as though he knew some secret that she didn't.

"It's good that you want to change things," he said. "It tells me that you want to be here. That makes me happy."

Her great uncle's face brimmed with something beyond joy. It triggered a hive of buzzing suspicions. "But?"

"But what?"

Emelina had sighed, pushing back curls that had escaped from behind her ears with one hand and reaching for her glass of icy lemonade with the other. They were on the porch of the main house where Rafa's son had set up two white wicker chairs side-by-side with a small table between them, allowing them to survey the immaculate rows of mahogany and imperial palms that lined the drive up to the main road.

"Lito," Emelina persisted. "You are an intelligent man,

right? And so was Papa Diego. So there must be some reason why you haven't cultivated anything else on the estate."

Ernesto broke into a laugh loud enough to echo in the empty house behind them.

"You are just like the woman you are named for, sabes? So direct, so quick to find gaps." He reached across to squeeze Emelina's shoulder. "Yes, pequeña, I'm not a silly old man, but, like my father, I'm a sentimental one. You see, our ancestor, Soñada, raised pigs. I've told you that, right?"

Emelina nodded.

"He didn't really buy the land for crops, for commercial farming. He liked his pigs to run free, he liked them to run wild. That's why our estate is the only one in this province that looks more like a forest reserve than a plantation.

"Of course, he planted corn and frijoles and vegetables but that was just for the family. But, really, this estate was for his pigs. Right there," Ernesto pointed to the rice paddies to the right of them. "He used to roast whole hogs by the dozen and the meat was cut, bagged and delivered all over Fumaz. Where the workers' quarters are, just by your cabin, there used to be a curing house for making ham. This place was for pigs and even though we no longer raise them, we didn't have the heart to change it, to clear the trees to plant peppers or onions. That's all. Just sentimental."

"So you don't object to my changing things?"

"Me? No, I don't," said Ernesto. "And, remember, it's your estate now. The rice is for us all, but the estate is yours.

The echo of the phone's click persisted as she pondered his words.

"They are coming today. I will speak to you later."

By USAs standards, the vehicle Rafa pointed her to, parked in the semi-circular driveway in front of the main house, was humble. A brown four-wheel drive with black windows. As she reached it, the rear door closest to her opened with a slow whine. She peered inside and could only make out a glint of the metal frames of some sunglasses.

"Come inside," said the voice behind the sunglasses.

Without her abuelo Ernesto's phone call, Emelina would have been hesitant; she'd heard enough stories from her grandfather in USAs to know that this must be the secret police. She climbed into the back seat, finding it surprisingly cool. The door closed behind her as though a phantom wind had followed her.

When her eyes adjusted to the dim interior, she made out a man with military shoulders in a dark green shirt. He offered his hand. "I am the Agriculture Minister," he said in a low voice, its tone pitched as though he carried unbearable loads, and she should know the weight of his worries.

Emelina was stunned to find that it was a highly ranked government official that had called on her, but she hid her surprise with a wide smile. "I am Emelina Soñada Santos."

She didn't know why she added Soñada as she introduced herself, but it made her feel more at ease.

"Así," the man said. "You are real family."

"Yes, I am."

"My name is Manuel Ortega. I am from a family of musicians and sportsmen." He opened his palms as though to add gravitas to his claimed heritage. "And… can I call you Emelina?"

She nodded.

"Bueno. Gracias. Entonces, although I studied agriculture and I do this job, I still honour my family traditions. Every month, on the last weekend, my family meets to play some baseball, to run, to eat and to sing.

"And, claro, I have a guitar in my house. Every evening when I go home, I play a song that my grandfather used to sing to us – a song he composed himself. When I visit my daughter at the weekend, sabes, I play it to my granddaughter. Traditions," he said, closing his palms.

"Family traditions are important," Emelina agreed, mildly disoriented by the many turns the conversation seemed to be taking.

Manuel sighed. "Then why are you planning to destroy yours?"

"I don't understand."

"Why do you wish to end production of Soñada Santos rice?"

Emelina laughed, relieved. "No. We are not ending production; we just won't be cultivating it here at Asadon any more."

The minister shook his head. "But this is where Soñada Sun started; this is where is belongs. It should be cultivated here."

"But there is no point. We barely produce enough for a small village here. What's the point in keeping up the illusion of producing here?"

The minister sighed again, a more resolute sound this time. "Illusion," he said, "is the cornerstone of life. If we don't have the story of Diego Soñada Santos reacting to the USAs embargo on our exports by watering his rice paddies with sugar, creating the sweetest rice in the world, of what value is the rice? Claro, even Fumaz, the whole country, loses something.

"Sabes, illusion is also the foundation of hope. This is what the Capitalites didn't understand when we started the struggle. A nation rises and falls on the hopes of its masses, entiendes? What worked in a capitalite country, like USAs, is that the people with the wealth and success look like the majority of the people. That alone has been enough to give hope to the masses that they can also attain the same status – especially those that do not look like the poorer, the darker, minority. Here, the people with wealth looked very different from the masses, who, like you and me…" Here the minister paused to rub the back of his revolutionary hand, the left one, with a neatly manicured finger. "…like you and me, have ancestors from Africa."

"The revolution worked because we didn't try to sell our people the dream in the same way. We said that all the masses could be as educated as the ones with wealth – and for free. That they could attend the same concerts, learn the same ballet… The idea that they can belong to the same club as the educated and the cultured makes our masses believe that they can be equal in all ways. That's the key to our version of popleism. We sell the masses on education, entiendes? But they see wealth because our wealthy are educated. That's the power of illusion; that's the engine of hope. And that hope is so powerful that it makes reality of the illusion. Look at how many painters, scientists, musicians, sportspeople and dancers we have produced through our free programmes, that now belong to a global club of excellence. Es maravilloso, no?

"Let me put it another way. You and I only know we are our parents' children because they tell us so. Not many people in the world demand a test to prove where they belong. But think of all the hopes founded on what could well be an illusion – the eternal hope of unconditional love, the expected communion of siblings, the idea of a country that will welcome us no matter where our families have strayed between the birth of a grandmother or father, and our own adulthood. The lure of hope erases the illusion that precedes it; when the illusion is exposed there is heartbreak.

"It is the same with your rice, me entiendes; people need to believe that when they buy Soñada Sun, the rice has been touched by the legend of its origins. It is one of this island's most powerful legends. Even the capitalite nations have not been able to resist it. It's a beautiful story. A story of love."

The minister clasped his hands and leaned back, his shoulders rising to embrace a huge intake of breath.

Emelina listened, staring at her hands, her mind drifting in and out of reverie. The minister's measured thesis intermingled with images of men in camouflage carving hearts into the barks of trees; tobacco drying in even racks, bloodying the horizon; amorous girls smuggling food beneath their skirts to feed men committed to dying; bar fights, afros, refuge centres and a wooden dance floor in Club 4381. Was it her mother's stories that fuelled the endurance of her hope or was it the nature of her memories? Illusion surely lurked in the story of desperate love between her star-crossed grandparents who lived in the blue hills. It all sounded like an idealised dream anyway. But then didn't every story build from illusion? Maybe that was the point the minister was trying to make; she was being too pragmatic, she needed to allow dreams a place in her life.

"But," she said. "And this is God's truth – the soil is so bad now that I don't think any rice will grow after this harvest."

Manuel broke into a smile. "What's the secret? I've always wanted to know."

"What secret? Everyone knows that we water our rice with sugar solution. It's the myth you have been talking about…"

"But are there sugar pipes in the soil?"

It was possible to see in the minister's animated posture the boy that he was before his shoulders turned so disciplined.

Emelina smiled in spite of herself. "No, it's not pipes. I can't tell you how. But the soil is saturated with sugar now; the rice can't grow.

"Oh!" exclaimed Manuel Ortega, Agriculture Minister, removing his sunglasses. He raised his chin and closed his eyes as though summoning his possibly illusory forebears on the West African coast for divine help.

"I know a man," he said finally. "I know a man."

"You think he can help the rice grow?"

"I think, yes," confirmed Manuel. "He is an experienced agriculturist. The problem is that he doesn't work anymore... but he is from this area, sabes, from Bana... so maybe I can convince him."

He put his sunglasses back on and turned to Emelina. "Thank you for considering our request. I will be in touch personally to let you know if I manage to convince Yunior to come and help with the Soñada Sun project."

He nodded and held out his hand. "A good day to you."

Emelina took his cue, shook his hand and stepped out of the vehicle, leaving Manuel Ortega in the dark. A blast of heat and humidity hit her in the face. It was high noon. The sun was as bright as it had ever been. She shielded her eyes and walked towards her cabin to find shade, to discover what solace the ghosts had found.

AGUANA

Let us return to music and to the harbour. Not the West Harbour, now the heart of Aguana Vieja, where Roberto Soñada first found fortune in the outpourings of citrus fruits, where the old food tables have transformed into restaurants in which tourists lose money in the gaps between what locals and visitors pay for food. No longer serving from fly-bejewelled pots of black beans, the restaurants are hives of multilingual chatter and parrot-coloured cocktails.

The transformation of the East Harbour, former enclave of vagabonds and pirates, is even more stunning. Its hourly chorus of fistfights has been replaced by the melodies emerging from the high-ceilinged storehouses long converted to live music clubs. It is in one of these, a place called Huaringas, that Yunior and Marcos have become known as Ayu Dante, a singer-songwriter duo playing original music in a style reminiscent of a stripped-down Pablo Milanés – without the pipes and violins and horns – and performed with the energy and percussive drive of Diomedes Díaz or Fumaz's own queen of rhythm, Quinta Aymaco. Playing either his guitar or the portable Korg CX3 organ he bought on his last trip away from Fumaz, Yunior sings of love and loss and everyday joys, with Marcos lending his gravelly alto to the choruses and dictating infectious rhythms on his drums. Yunior had first started playing by himself, not telling any of his bandmates about the music he played when he was not with them. Inevitably, however, Marcos, who played with many bands in Aguana when they needed a fill-in drummer, saw Yunior opening for a band from Ecuador and waited for him backstage.

"You are an idiot, Yunior," he said, slapping his friend's chest and pushing him backwards.

Yunior smiled. "I'm glad you caught me. I didn't know how to tell you guys that I was trying something new."

His response was only half true. While he had grown confident playing the Hammond organ in the privacy of the outhouse or the Korg through headphones at home in Aguana, Yunior didn't feel ready to face his musician friends, so he'd actively sought music clubs where he didn't expect anyone he knew to turn up. The other harbour, closer to the centre of Aguana and in the vicinity of Hípica, the club where the band often played, was where established musicians played. The Eastern Harbour was where up-and-coming singers, touring bands and experimental acts performed. He was going into the unknown, but he was undeterred. His mother had on occasion compared his ambition to the habits of lizards. "Provide a shade," she'd say "and lizards will come." Ruffling his hair, she'd add, "but your shade is challenge. You always want to do what you are told you can't." In a world of words, all those feelings, doubts and a mother's observation translate to a long silence and a smile when you are caught out.

Marcos shook his head. "You sound good, hermano, but you're an idiot! Did no one tell you that if you play love songs with no drums, you'll make people feel low? You're lucky you only did three songs. If you were the headliner there would be misery in this place."

Yunior laughed, placing an arm around Marcos's shoulder. "Is that an offer to play with me?"

"¡Pero por supuesto! But your organ playing... I don't want to ask." Marcos clapped once, as though killing a mosquito. "Es caliente, hijo... estupendo!"

Ayu Dante was born in that July moment, in the lull that

149

follows the tourist season, when musicians can relax in the shadows of the old brothels of the East Harbour, where many of the city's secrets had their roots. Yunior and Marcos found liberty and joy in their collaboration; it was something they could explore even when they visited each other, with only a cajón and a guitar needed to play around with ideas.

They still played with Los Puntos Estelares on Fridays and Saturdays, at Hípica on the other side of the split hand that led to the wrist of Aguana's sea, finding an ever-growing crowd of faithful fans flocking to experience their infectious sound. "Vivimos Juntos" had become something of an anthem in Fumaz; dancers actually paused the relentless motion of their bodies to turn towards the stage and sing along when the band played this song. And when the seed of disposability sown in José led him to join a new band, Yunior often played the keyboards when they couldn't find someone to fill in. It seemed easier to find a guest to sit in on guitar. This island of ours has more guitarists than fireflies.

Even so, they went through a catalogue of guitarists as the month ticked off its days; thin and stubby fingered, sullen and smiling, granddaughters and grandfathers, suricate-nervous and reptile-serene, drink-fuelled and smoke-driven, skilled, struggling, muted and loud. But none of them was compatible enough to make themselves the kind of fixture José had become before he left. Still, as they had played without a steady guitarist for much of the time when Yunior was in mourning, the changes were not too disruptive for the rest of the band, but for Yunior, who was used to hearing the guitar elements of their songs, it was disorienting, and he hoped that they would find a stable player soon. Occasionally he switched between instruments, but clearly without George they could not reproduce the sublime *sui generis* sound of the original five.

The stirrings of August altered the winds stealing into the harbours. Walking past the girls and boys casting fishing lines into the lapping waters of the Malecón, Marcos told Yunior that a guitarist called Manuel would play with them on Saturday. Marcos's daughter, elevated above her usual world, secure on her father's shoulders, sang bright, clear notes along the route to the food market. Yunior clapped a rhythm for her, content in the borrowed domesticity of the moment. In that school holidays' sliver of time, walking alongside his bandmate, preparing for a cookout with friends in the gregarious Aguana sun, how was Yunior to know that Manuel was Manuel Ortega, Agriculture Minister? It was simply another of many layers of information, a sub-octave of the day's amalgamated chord.

So when Yunior saw the man sitting at the bar in Hípica on Saturday, he merely saw his old boss sipping a snifter.

"Colonel Ortega," he shouted, knowing full well that the man did not like to be addressed by his military title.

He had only been in the army for six months and his high ranking was simply because he was a high-ranking guerrilla converted into an army officer as Rosario assumed office. As a fresh-faced 18-year-old, he used blades in battle before he ever had reason to put one to his own face to trim his beard. He had gained widespread fame for holding up a military garrison and munitions depot starting with no more than an unripe plantain pressed strategically into the back of a guard, thus earning the nickname Plátano. The name announced his incarnation as a rebel and established his lifelong link to agriculture; in other areas of cultivation, he left a scattering of broken hearts in the green belly of our hinterland.

Comrade Plátano had gone straight into university and graduated three years later as an agriculturist. He began fieldwork for the Ministerio de Agricultura, continuing his mission of heartbreaking, with his guitar in tow, his string-callused fingers igniting fires on the skins of farm girls. The heartbreaking had, however, stopped at the feet of a young Eva Portas, a woman made entirely of fire and fruit.

The minister stood and took Yunior's hand. "Yunior. You look well."

"Thank you, Colonel. As do you."

The older man's face hardened momentarily, before he cracked a smile and sat back down. "Call me Manuel," he winked, picking up his snifter of rum and swirling the dark liquid before taking a sip.

In that flick of the minister's wrist, it dawned on Yunior why the man was there. He wasn't a high-ranking official of the government allowed in early to witness the band rehearse; he was going to be part of the rehearsal. He was the Manuel that Marcos had met playing at a small fiesta the week before and had asked to join Los Puntos on stage.

"You never mentioned that you played, Manuel."

The minister shook his head. "Actually, I did. We spoke about music and baseball."

"You were a lot calmer than I was at the time," Yunior smiled. "I remembered the baseball."

"I guess tonight will be the turn of the music."

"OK," Marcos yelled from across the room. "Let's rehearse."

In the middle of their first break, Manuel mentioned that he might need Yunior's help for an agricultural project.

"But, you know, I'm not working anymore," said Yunior.

"I know, Yunior." Manuel paused. "I understand."

Yunior picked up his Balboa beer and walked back to his stool behind the piano.

Manuel trailed Yunior with a refilled snifter of rum, taking his position between Yunior and Esperanza, just behind the monitors at the front of the stage. He plucked his D string, cocking his head to the left until the sound crossed into the realm of silence, then he tightened the string slightly.

Yunior leaned towards the minister. "You sounded great on "Interrupción". It's good to play with you."

Manuel cradled the body of his guitar closer. "It would be a one-off," he whispered. "It's not really a return to work, entiendes? It's a complete one-off – complete one-off."

Yunior glanced at the older man, admiring the undiminished tenacity of his will. Though in his early sixties, he retained the enthusiasm of a fourteen-year-old. Yunior's gaze shifted backwards, catching the movement of Marcos's hands. His drumsticks were aloft, a sign that he was about to count the band off to start their second set. As Yunior flexed his fingers and shifted on the stool, Manuel spoke again.

"It's at the Soñada Santos estate, near your home in Bana."

Marcos's drumsticks sliced through the air, settling into the cradle of an opening beat. Music swirled, the propulsive rhythm lifting everything it struck, opening a clear pathway for lyrics.

Yunior adjusted his microphone stand to angle the silver dome of its windscreen closer to his lips and caught Esperanza's eye with a smile. Thoughts of the açaí palms on the Soñada Santos estate, the mystery of that grand, empty house and the sweet myth of its sugar-drenched paddies circled his mind as he crooned the new Los Puntos Estelares song into the microphone, in flawless synch with Esperanza's spiky alto – the lyrics, part confession, part defiance, part history, part fortune-telling: *Yo no sé, porque te amo, pero sé que no puedo luchar*.

Marcos and Manjate injected their percussive arguments beneath the skin of the song's lament. Manuel Ortega of silvering temples, agriculture minister, guerrilla, lover of fruit and fire, sportsman, musician and rum-drinker, put his fingers to work along the guitar strings. In the verse, his chords initially hovered over the melody, then ducked beneath its shadows; he plucked notes into the crevices of the chorus's twists, his touch light as a lover's on wet skin riddled with goosebumps, getting firmer as the refrain bloomed with the desperation of restrained passion. By the time Marcos cued him in for his solo, Comrade Plátano was lost in the heart of the song, knife in hand, tattooing his imprint on the bark of its sound. It was though he had been with the band his whole life.

ASADON

The sun's departing protest breaks through the gaps in the trees to illuminate the route to Asadon. As the brown official vehicle pulls into the semi-circular driveway, Yunior feels a worm of excitement wriggling under his skin at the thought of finally stepping into the old house. Beneath the worm linger muted musings on his last – and first – visit to the estate with Loretta.

The thud of Manuel Ortega's door closing propels him out of his thoughts. As Yunior gets out of the car, Rafa, who is taking their bags from the back seats, nods at him with a hint of recognition. Yunior follows Manuel up the stairs to the main house's verandah.

Emelina Soñada Santos stands at the top of the stairs waiting for them. Her hair, held up in an untidy bun, filters what's left of the light behind her, through follicles that contain all her family history in their helices. The diffused orange strikes both men in the eyes.

Manuel Ortega greets her with two swift kisses on each cheek and turns to introduce her to his companion.

"Yunior, this is Emelina Soñada Santos, the owner of the estate; Emelina, Yunior. The man we spoke about."

Yunior takes Emelina's hand and performs a playful bow. "Encantado." He is struck by the sense of familiarity you feel when you encounter a smell that conjures memories of a dish from your grandparent's kitchen that you never saw but knew very well by its aromas.

Emelina smiles and, using a thumb, gestures behind her, where the house stands. "I hope you don't mind that you'll be staying in the old house. It's not like it used to be, it's virtually empty, but it's clean, the beds have been…"

"It's perfect," Yunior interrupts. "We don't need much." He is actually more excited about exploring the house as an empty shell, hearing its wooden echo, calibrating his imagined experience of it against the real smell and grain of its history.

"Yes, yes. We're fine," agrees Manuel.

"Can I see the paddies?" Yunior asks. "I'd like to take a handful of the wet loam."

"OK," says Emelina. She is hesitant. He doesn't look much like a miracle worker with his close-cropped beard and hair. However, there is the minister, of silvering temples, standing beside him, nodding his approval. She does not feel she can refuse.

In a clear glass, the mud from the paddy has a hue close to that of Yunior's skin – dark brown with a queer sheen that hints at vibrant life. It has the skin tone of Fumaz's Taíno, descending blue hills with smiles, to be betrayed, slaughtered, infected with diseases, raped, pushed back into green; it has the rebellious brown of the Mambíses in the jungle, hidden and emergent only at their will; the shade of kidnapped women who walked miles barefoot, threatened by whips, still carrying songs beneath their tongues, stamping harmonies in the undergrowth; it has the many-grained texture of men shackled from Africa, hair matted and plaited into triangular partitions on the scalp, kinks recording the turns and betrayal of history; it has the uneven skin of maids making family, weaving wholes from what was broken. It is the colour of heritage. It is the colour of sweet molasses, of unbalmed bruises. It possesses the granularity of families beaten by harmattan sand while queuing for food in a Sahel-sent drought. It has the same sick, sinking weight as flesh, the density of struggle, of blood.

Yunior lifts the glass to the lamp hanging above them, where they sit around a corner of the grand dining table, forming an uneven triangle.

"It's certainly saturated," he says. "Feel the weight of it."

He passes the glass around and when it returns to him he takes a pinch of its contents and places it on his tongue.

Emelina's face, angles accentuated by the proximity of the light, can't conceal her disgust. She has learned to forget the time when she had dirt in her mouth; attacked on the Sun Coast as other Fumazero – pale, pale Fumazero, unwilling to break the cover that allowed them to pass as USAs – watched and did nothing. Watching Yunior brings it all back.

"I'd say the sugar content has been elevated by evaporation," says Yunior. "It's very close to a saturated solution with soil thrown in."

Manuel leans forward, taking a pinch of mud himself and rubbing it between two fingers. "So, sabes, is there a solution?"

"It's safe to taste it, Colonel. At our daytime temperatures, you've probably got two grammes per millilitre of sugar in there – even staphylococcus wouldn't survive it. However, she's right."

Yunior lifts the glass towards Emelina, but she shakes her head.

"There is no way rice will continue to grow in there; I'm surprised there is any growing now, even though it looks like you grow a very hardy variety that comes from West Africa – probably a vestige of the slave trade. I'm guessing that the locally collected seeds have adapted to the sugar content of the soil. Plants are not so different from us; they find ways to settle, to survive, to belong."

Emelina looks at Manuel and shrugs.

Manuel turns to Yunior. "So there's nothing that can be done?"

"I don't think so. Even with the evolved seeds, you definitely wouldn't be able to water with a sugar solution." He holds out a palm in the direction of Manuel. "You said that was important, right?"

Emelina shifts in her chair, less sceptical of Yunior now that she has seen him at work, now that she has heard him speak about plants with an ache of reverence and wonder.

"I already explained that we are able to produce rice that tastes the same at our other farms," she interjects. "But he keeps talking about mythology."

Yunior laughs. "It would be a myth for me to tell you that you can grow rice in that soil as it is. Even vetiver would barely grow in there."

"So that's it?"

"I'm afraid so," says Yunior.

Manuel Ortega lifts the glass, staring at the soil in it as though it carries answers in its depths. Light refracts through the lens of its crystal base.

"Do you mind showing me around properly before you leave us?" Yunior stands and waits next to Emelina's chair. "I might as well make this visit count."

Emelina takes his hand, steadying herself as she stands too. "Why not? What do you want to see?"

Yunior smiles, noting that Emelina has not let go of his hand, but feeling no inclination to be the one to break the hold. "I always imagined a large drawing room when driving past. Is there one?"

Emelina laughs out loud, her open-mouthed explosion resonating in the hollows of the house. The return the walls give on her sound lends her ballast and she feels connected to this house in a way she has never felt before tonight, a way she didn't feel when Abuelo Ernesto was showing her around, explaining the nooks, the eccentric collections of curios, the rooms added on as afterthoughts, the paintings, pictures and handmade bits of furniture. The resonance of the house is an embrace, it is love in sound.

"Well, your imagination is pretty accurate," she says. "We do have one – and it's where all the history is stored actually – portraits, contracts…"

She tugs at Yunior's hand. "Come with me."

Her tugging has an openness, he thinks, born of assumed transience, belief in the brevity of the connection creating intimacy.

The minister doesn't know whether he should join them and remains where he is.

The first thing to catch Yunior's attention is the small, raised stage at the end of the room, directly opposite the large doorway they walk through, with French doors behind it, making it possible to have a musician on the stage playing for guests inside as well as outside. He visualises trios, bailarines de son, quartets, ballets, tap dancers… alive in that space.

Emelina pulls him to the right, where the wall features a display of Soñada Santos ancestry.

"The ones here are the newest ones," she says, pointing at a series of fine pencil sketches, preceding a succession of photographs that improve in clarity as they move further away from the French doors. With a few exceptions, all the backgrounds in the drawings are of trees and cultivated fields, with one or more persons in the foreground. The first, however, is of an elegantly dressed man beside a dappled pig.

"That is Soñada," says Emelina. "He started all of this; he bought all the land the estate stands on. The pig is called Luchando."

"He looks like an uncle of mine," Yunior says.

"The pig?" Emelina asks with a sparkle in her eye.

Yunior laughs, wagging a finger at her.

"Well, it's an artist's impression. The pig was dead before he owned anything significant."

She winks. "Maybe your uncle posed for it? Manuel said you're from Bana."

"He couldn't have." Yunior shakes his head. "My uncle lives in Ghana."

Emelina hesitates, as though she wants to ask a question, then she moves to the next picture. "This is Sergio, the oldest of Soñada's sons. He worked with his father here on the farm, raising pigs and making ham before he became a dealer in knives and kitchen utensils."

Yunior frowns, looking a little ahead at the sketches of Soñada's twelve children. "How come the women are all darker than the men?"

"The men all had different mothers – only Soñada knew who they were, but they were European. The five women were all by his wife, Maria. The oldest – the one there –" Emelina points at a tall woman sketched in front of an açaí palm, balancing a tray in one hand – "she was also named Maria. She made cakes and sweets."

Yunior returns to stand close to Emelina and she smiles.

"This is Roberto Soñada; he was the first to sell rice in the family and the first to move to Aguana. He was the father of the woman I'm named after – Emelina. She's my favourite."

She moves to the first of the photographs. "Emelina moved from Aguana to help her aunt Maria with her catering and ended up staying here. She's the one who built this house – the main house – and started the rice fields. She bought the camera that was used for most of these photographs too – 1911; the first in Fumaz. She loved gadgets."

Yunior is fascinated by the photograph. There is the striking resemblance between Emelina and her namesake, of course, but it is the object beside her that has him entranced. It's a copper distillation still.

Emelina moves back to the pencil sketches, her arm casually linked with Yunior's. "And this is Juan. My father is named after him..."

Yunior stops, takes Emelina's hand and pulls her a few steps forward, back to the photograph.

She is unsure why he is pulling her towards him, but experiences a brief sensation of adventure, a feeling not unlike what her first trip to Fumaz gave her, an inexplicable hankering after the unknown. Time slows down, she can feel the individual pads of his fingers, the throb of blood inside them, hardened ends that puzzle her. She is certain she can hear cicadas outside, a chorus in the quiet, quiet night.

Yunior points at the photograph of Emelina, his finger tapping at the precise spot inhabited by the distillation still. "Was this taken here?" he asks.

"I'm fairly sure. The camera never left the estate; it's still in that cabinet over there." She points across the room, to a mass of shelved curios trapped behind framed glass doors.

"So, this still might be here?" He taps the spot again.

Emelina frowns, trying to imagine where such a thing might be. She had visited the curing house after speaking to her abuelo Ernesto. It was a large space, but empty except for an assembly of wooden barrels and the hooks still dangling on beams for hanging ham.

"There's a large pantry behind the kitchen," she offers, eventually. "It's probably there. She used to make fruit liqueurs."

"Good," he says. "Do you bake?"

"Actually, I do," she smiles.

"Great!" He puts his hands on her shoulders as though he's preparing her for a photograph and absent-mindedly nudges a coil of hair away from her forehead. He is alive with a restless energy. "Wait here," he says, and runs back to the dining room, where Manuel Ortega still lingers.

He returns with Manuel in tow, virtually dragging the minister after him. Yunior is silently grateful for the thoroughness of his agricultural production classes in university. He was one of the students that used to question why they had to learn the basics of pasteurisation and canning and distillation and curing, when their primary duties would be to increase production on farms – not processing or packaging.

Yunior stops in front of the photograph of Emelina Soñada and points at the still. "We may have a solution," he says.

Manuel Ortega has made a life out of remaining inscrutable. To take a garrison lookout's weapon off him with a green plátano takes guts and a face that reads like a rock. But now he can't hide his bewilderment. "¿Qué?"

Yunior speaks so fast that it is hard to follow at first, then it all becomes clear. He thinks they can distil rum from the mud. Since the Soñada Santos estate uses a cane sugar solution on the paddies, what is in the mud is the same raw material used to make rum. Once the sugar is leached out to make rum, they can repack the soil, revitalise it with worms and a season of legumes, and return to planting rice. If they start now, they can work on the land in sections every six months so that rice production doesn't have to stop. He wants them to find the small still from the photograph, ferment some mud solution and distil it to test his idea.

"There is some native yeast in the loam anyway; there's a hint of alcohol in it," he says. "But some yeast from your baking will make it quicker to ferment. It will still take just over a week and a half, of course!"

He turns to Manuel. "Colonel, you're an experienced rum drinker. You can be our taste tester, our own connoisseur."

The minister chuckles, shaking his head. "You think this will work?"

Yunior smiles. "It's better than nothing, right? Let's just say it will be an exciting few days."

He claps and hugs both Emelina and Manuel.

"Right, where were we?" Yunior says, walking towards the last set of pictures, near the side-stage grand piano that catches more light than the room can give, dappled with doses of the moonlight streaming through the French doors.

Emelina woke from what was supposed to be a light siesta to find the red glow of sunset licking the faces of the cabin's walls. The exhaustion of the last week had trailed her in secret and finally claimed its arrears. It wasn't just her role in the frantic quest to make Soñada rum that had tired her; she had found that she couldn't pull back from the familiarity she had built with Yunior on the first night, and while it felt good to talk with someone with such ease, it was also odd because they had only known each other for ten days, so she often felt as if she was on stage – it was draining. She stared up at the ceiling beams that her great-grandfather's hands had placed, thinking that the tree the beams came from probably had a facsimile in the forest sentried on the eastern horizon of the estate.

In the cycle of flower, fruit, seed, soil, seedling, tree, the wood never lost its heritage; there was a characteristic grain and hue when it was planed that only it possessed. Even if the seed were carried to another Caribbean island, even to Ecuador – or further – in the bowels of a fine-feathered bird, or by gentle currents to germinate alone, it would still belong to a genus, a family. It would also become a tree of the new land, adapting to its climate, its cycles, the impacts of its leaders' decisions – bearded or not, deluded or cogent.

Yunior's monologues on plants had become part of her daily routine in the past week. He had spoken mainly of rum and soil; testing for clay content and acidity, worrying about maintaining temperatures in the sugar wash, watching the frijoles soften – as we say on this island of ours. But as the process settled, his conversation shifted to music, food – even politics! His commentary on leaders was cheeky, almost daring given that they had been in the company of the Agriculture Minister, but it was pitched perfectly – as though he knew intimately the limits one could flirt with in Fumaz.

In the last two days, with Manuel Ortega gone, Emelina had realised that Yunior spoke like that all the time. He hadn't been teasing the minister. She had caught herself staring at his lips several times and she made a face thinking about it. She stared at her own dark hands, planted in USAs but a mirror of her Fumaz ancestor's, pondering the meaning of having the same name – tied together a century apart.

As she pulled on some fresh clothes for dinner, she was sure she could hear the tinkling of the grand piano from the main house, a mix of a hesitant assembly of notes with confident passages. She straightened the thin orange straps of her dress, a smile light on her face, content with the idea of the grand house Emelina Soñada built filled again with music and chatter.

Engrossed in his quest to fuse three pieces of music into a pleasing whole, Yunior didn't notice Emelina standing in the main entrance to the drawing room, her hair out and fading from red halo to blackness in the last dregs of sunlight. He had abandoned his guitar, Omarita, on the edge of the stage next to the grand piano, determined to make the most of the chance to explore a new sound. He played with restraint, like a refugee seeking opportunity, a stranger at a dance class, but his ponderous approach had its roots in an urge to interpret rather than a lack of confidence.

None of the pieces he was playing was written for piano. "L'amant anonyme", the opening he has started with, was written for violin. Yunior had fashioned a pleasing progression of chords, runs and embellishments to convey the composition's beauty, but he'd found it a little melancholy for his mood. He'd tried to enliven it with borrowings from the percussive opening to A.B. Crentsil's "Moses", a song that opened with a meditation on not worrying that he found particularly resonant at the moment. However, both passages were of slow to moderate tempo, so he'd infused some presto from the overture to *The Marriage of Figaro*, which he was using as a sort of pop chorus. Yunior smiled as it came together, finally, a confident new hybrid exuberantly alive. He'd felt a sudden urge to replicate his invention on Omarita and turned towards the stage, catching a flash of Emelina's dress in the corner of his eye.

Emelina applauded, walking slowly towards him.

Yunior kissed her on both cheeks, then stood back, frowning. "So you're a spy now, ¿verdad?"

Emelina laughed, slapping his arm playfully. "No, I just didn't want to interrupt. It sounded familiar but I couldn't place it."

"It's not a real song. You probably recognised the Mozart." Yunior hummed the overture to *The Marriage of Figaro*. "It's from an opera."

"Yes, I know that one. What else was there?"

"A song from Ghana called "Moses" and something from a CD my younger brother recently gave me, also from an opera. The composer is called Joseph Bologne; he was a violinist, fencer and soldier in the 18th Century."

"¿Es un fanático de la ópera, tu hermano?"

Yunior chuckled. "He's a fan of anything he doesn't know. He speaks six languages, knows about Songhai empire rivalries, Indian spices and Italian art – that kind of thing. He's studying in France at the moment, wants to be a diplomat."

"He sounds fascinating."

"He is." Yunior nodded, his gaze drifting to the deepening dusk outside, lost in thought. He sat on the edge of the stage, picking up his guitar. "Estoy nervioso."

"What are you nervous about?" She lowered herself to sit beside him, leaning back on her elbows to look at him sideways.

"I like challenges and I love working to improve the lives of our people. That's what I loved about the first project I worked on for the government."

He rubbed the body of Omarita, as though soothing the guitar, then put it down. "It's a bit like what I just helped to start, sabes, with the vegetables. It was just around *half-time* and it helped thousands in the cities to feed themselves. That was a great project. But this is political."

"You think our rice is political?"

"Oh sí, it's as political as the Cubans and their cigars. It's political because its existence and the global demand for it enhances the reputation of our government. But, for me, it's also political because it reveals the flaw in all political systems; there is always an elite that is not materially affected by the chess games that governments play.

"Quiero decir, everybody talks about embargoes and we suffer the consequences here, but our leaders can still get what they need. Your family sells Soñada Santos rice..."

"Soñada Sun," Emelina interjected.

"Sí, Soñada Sun, officially in USAs. It is served at official banquets there and yet they have had an embargo in force against us for forty odd years. Cuba's Cohiba cigars are smoked all over the world – everywhere I've played a concert I've seen it."

Emelina sighed, unsure what to say. Abuelo Ernesto had been very forthright about their family being privileged and how, in the end, her grandfather Elián being in USAs, publicly declaring his opposition to Rosario, had in fact helped them weather the fluctuations of Fumaz's local economy. Keen to use Elián as a poster boy for Fumazero resistance, USAs had actively supported his business, his lifestyle and – by extension – the financial security of the entire Soñada Santos clan. But she also knew that their wealth was not the same kind of wealth as many of the other Fumazero who lived on the Sun Coast, the kind of Fumazero who had watched her eat dirt. The Soñada fortune was a fortune of self-sacrifice and sweat, not built off the backs of labour bought at the market. Besides, it was the fortune that had saved her mother, one of the less privileged Fumazero, from a life that already had her in the USAs social care system, the fate that had rescued the space in Alae's life reserved for the love of dance and music. But perhaps music was as ingrained in her mother as the thread and sap of struggle in Fumaz's scarred, unyielding trees.

"So music is not just a hobby for you? You're a professional?"

Yunior laughed. "Music is the foundation of my life. Didn't Manuel tell you?"

He picked up Omarita. "Let me play you something," he said, plucking the bottom E string, letting it fill the hollows of the grand drawing room before he shaped a D chord. "This is called 'Sometimes on a Roof'."

Yunior closed his eyes and hummed his way into the contours of the song. He followed its lines as it meandered through the streets of Aguana, his mouth opening to render in words the breathless feeling of a beer bottle's sweat on your shoulder, pulling you fast and headlong into the mysteries of sunset views of rock and sea cove. In the melody's undertow, the ping of strings pulled between chords, there was the whirl and swirl of international politics, the crouch of enamoured youths under the incandescence of luminous moths and fireflies, the treachery of ghosts and pancreatic cancer. Beneath the chorus was the yawn of death, the red-eyed fatigue and fading yellow sunflower inertia that followed, the bellow of loneliness, a voice echoing in a room of notes.

When Yunior finished there were pearls gleaming on his face. Emelina, herself in the vortex of her mother's losses, heartaches and nostalgia, her breath uneven from the pace of the music's quest, could summon no words for the moment. She reached over and wiped Yunior's face using a single finger as though it would be less intrusive.

Yunior caught the finger and placed her hand in her lap. "Lo siento," he said. "I didn't mean to cry."

Emelina made a swift smile that seemed uncertain of its emotion and moved her arm back to where it was before, anchoring her reclining torso.

Yunior pulled Omarita closer to his chest. "Believe it or not, that song was about the second project I worked on for the government."

"But the woman…" Emelina's brow bunched like crushed paper. "The woman in the song."

He nodded. "She's real. She died six months ago. She was carrying our baby. Loretta."

Emelina felt an urge to hold him, but the guitar, solid in its heritage of wood and wind, was in the space where human warmth should be and he was holding it so tight, his dark hands turned to sculpture in the moonlight.

"She was the one who noticed that I play music when I have a dilemma, when I am thinking."

"So, this project is a dilemma?"

He laughed. "When the agriculture minister says, 'This spirit will have a unique flavour that speaks of the sugar's decades-long contact with the soil; this is a rum that could embody our struggles', yes."

Yunior turned to face Emelina, marking how the orange of her dress brought a feel of sunlight into the shadowed drawing room. "No, I'm joking. It's not so much the project; in spite of my peopleist reservations, I took on the project because everything I have been taught said that rescuing those paddies would be impossible; or as Profesor Blades – I worked with him on the last project – would say, im*probable*.

"My dilemma is the solution. Yes, if we manage to get some kind of rum from the soil, but the Colonel says it's bland, has no character… I can accept that. But for him to have to visit our famous rum distilleries to borrow something from them to help give your rum flavour…" He raised his shoulders. "No sé. I have a problem with that."

"I see," said Emelina. "So…"

Yunior put Omarita down on the stage, strings facing the floor, and paced the room. "I'm sorry. It's the whole myth thing he's been talking about – Manuel. If we are to buy into that, then everything about this rum, and the rice when the soil can produce again, must come from here – right here!"

Emelina suppressed a smile, amused by the spectacle of Yunior stamping on the floor as he said 'right here', with nothing but dimly lit images of her ancestry lined up behind him.

"Can I help?" she offered. "I mean history and myth are related, right? Sometimes it's hard to tell one from the other. I know the history of this place."

Yunior threw his hands in the air. "Yes, but this is about rum," he yelled, his voice carrying out of the drawing room, through the corridors, all the way to the dining room where their dinner waited, a place set for two.

Emelina moved from her reclining position, leaning forward on the stage. "So tell me more about rum."

"¡Dios mío!" Yunior laughed. "OK. From scratch?"

She nodded.

He approached the stage and squatted in front of Emelina. "You remember what we've been doing – the fermentation, the test distillation a few days ago…"

Emelina nodded.

"Well, with rum…" He shook his head. "Actually, with all

spirits, that is only the beginning. Only a part of the flavour comes from that process. I mean, already what we got from the early test has this earthy signature that the Colonel spoke about – something that no other rum can have. There is also the hardness and taint of the water. But to be distinct, spirits need to be aged. *Royal Brackla*, a famous Scottish whisky, was distilled in copper stills and aged in old sherry barrels. *Ron Barceló*, from the Dominican Republic is aged in fired white oak barrels; that, with the local temperature, humidity and the time it spends in the barrel, gives it a particular bouquet. Incluso, *Glenfiddich*, also Scottish, has some of its whisky aged in old rum barrels because whatever used to be in the barrels before affects the flavour."

"Is that why Manuel went away? To get barrels to age the rum in?"

"Why are you smiling?" Yunior asked.

"Answer me: is that why Manuel left?"

"Yes. To get a few old barrels from different distilleries so we can experiment to find one that will give us the best flavours when we age the alcohol we get from the earth in it. The problem is, ideally we'd get the barrels from somewhere else, like Portugal or Jamaica, which would be fine but because of our import regulations – and also some embargoes – we can't.

"For me, to take barrels from a distiller you will compete with doesn't make sense because..." He stopped mid-flow, placing his hands on Emelina's shoulders. "Why are you smiling?"

Emelina shook her head, her eyes liquid with bright mirth. In his squatting position, Yunior was half a head shorter than her, a principal in an orchestra looking up for guidance from the conductor.

"Well," Yunior stood up and folded his arms. "I am saying nothing more until you tell me."

"Just sit by me, por favor. I don't want you to stamp anymore."

Yunior frowned, then laughed at the image of himself stamping in the middle of the wooden floor with only this engaging woman, an assembly of family pictures and whatever dynasties of trees lurked in the dark distance for an audience.

"I'm sorry," he said, shaking his head as he lowered himself beside her.

"So," said Emelina. "Do you know much about making ham?"

He shrugged. "I know the theory; you rub the meat in salt, cover it in a curing mix – a salt-based mix with sugar and spices – cure it for a while in the mix and hang it."

She angled her head to one side. "Close. This is where my history might help you. Soñada had his own curing mix – it was salt, sugar… I think there was chilli and sage in it – and coriander seeds. Anyway, he made it in huge batches and stored it…

"Have you ever heard of *El Colón* rum?" She absent-mindedly put a hand on Yunior's thigh.

He laughed. "Now that, I know, is a myth. The story is that it was a rum made here in the middle to late 19th Century that the Spaniards used to fight over."

"See, I can confirm that rum existed – it is real history, not myth. I have seen a barrel that the rum was stored in."

"You've seen a barrel? Where?"

"Right here – on this estate."

Yunior looked like he wanted to stand again but was holding himself back. "Where?"

Emelina lifted a finger, a lone sapling in the storm of his brewing impatience. "And not just one. They had 41 barrels when they went out of business and Soñada bought all of them."

Yunior held both her hands. "Where?"

"Stacked in our curing house, near my cabin," Emelina said.

Yunior jumped up, pulling her with him as if he were taking her for a walk in the wilderness of his dreams. He pulsed with an energy that filled the shadowed room. He whooped, skipping erratically, then he stopped. "Wait. What did he keep in them?"

"The curing mix."

Yunior whooped again. "Azúcar, sal, chile, semillas de cilantro, salvia…" He kissed the air. "Flavours, flavours, flavours… Thank you!"

Emelina yelped as he lifted her in the air and spun her around, the orange bell of her dress making a whirlwind of the air around them.

"We need a song," he said, putting Emelina down with an old-world flourish, bowing as he retreated to pick up his guitar.

"Do you dance?" he asked.

"How dare you?" she fixed her fists on her waist and stared at him, feeling the room shrink. "I am Fumazero."

"OK," he laughed. He plucked a few familiar chords and winked at her. "Pacheco or Sanchez?"

"Alberto Sanchez," she said, stamping the way Yunior had a problem ago.

He bit his lower lip, trying not to laugh, but a chuckle escaped. "Good choice. Real Fumazero music."

Amusement still seeping from his skin, he played a Sanchez song, his voice edgy as it crept up the range of Alberto's paean to the northern hills.

Having grown up on the Isla de la Inocencia, off the coast of the Western Provinces, on the same side of the country where Emelina and Yunior stood on wooden floors beloved of the dancers of this beautiful island of ours, it was widely acknowledged that Sanchez's song was a tongue-in-cheek celebration of his lover's breasts. His talk of sugared lands that intoxicate had little to do with sugarcane and the noble art of distilling rum. Even our great leader of the liquid beard and engraved revolutionary expression couldn't keep up the act when the diminutive crooner sang at his 70th birthday. His waist caught the green and yellow fever of our island, proving that decades of paranoia, beard-growing and cleaning guns at the breakfast table can't steal your rhythm.

Emelina, in the moonlight once again, let the spirit of her playful dances with her mother inhabit her. Dancing around Yunior, she swayed and shimmied, singing along and acting out Sanchez's lyrics, shaking her northern hills, strutting and miming kisses at will.

Yunior played in a trance, feeling himself respond to Emelina's energy without reserve. As her dancing turned more dramatic, his mind went back to a night in Aguana almost five years ago – March 31st – when he'd watched a woman dance like that while he played on stage, her hair out and illuminated, her spirit free. He was now sure Emelina was the same woman. It was before Loretta, but he still remembered the feeling like it was a moment ago. His body was alight with certainty. He paused to take out his wallet, extracting a faded Big Green gum wrapper which he placed on the floor between them. Emelina barely glanced at it as Yunior segued into a chord progression that he could play half-dead. It was the first song he had written with Esperanza and Marcos, now an anthem in Fumaz.

Every note of it triggers a memory and the woman in a sleeveless blue dress dancing like a classic bailarine de son is one of them; so is the image of the Malecón, suddenly empty, leaving him alone under the street lamp.

As Yunior began to sing, Emelina froze, her eyes dark with recognition as they flitted between the wrapper on the floor and Yunior's face. Outside, the sky grew black above the rice paddies, sugar clung tight to soil and an entire assembly of peering trees whispered the story of the moment into the breeze, a tale that would grow in its own time and carry all the way to a gnarled olive on a roof in Aguana.

ACKNOWLEDGEMENTS

Although she doesn't know it, Niki Aguirre's joyful storytelling was a huge inspiration for starting this novel. I wanted to write a book in which wonder is always lurking – a feeling I get when reading Niki's work. So, I thank Niki, and I thank two lifetime rivals, Gabriel García Márquez and Mario Vargas Llosa who inspired the animation of the landscape in Azúcar.

Thanks to my agents David Godwin and Philippa Sitters for always believing in my strange fiction experiments, embracing a satire and romance hybrid without so much as a raised eyebrow. To my French and Spanish publishers – Editions Zulma and Club Editor – I owe a debt of gratitude for their faith in my craft and early encouragement with this book, and, of course Jeremy Poynting at Peepal Tree Press who saw the possibilities in the draft I sent him.

I am grateful to the Arts Council of England for supporting me to take time off to get this story started, to the Royal Literary Fund for placing me at the University of Aberystwyth where I was able to take basic Spanish classes for free, to the Civitella Ranieri Foundation who gave me much needed space to think and dream during a very difficult period in my personal life and to Berklee College of Music for making classes available online, enabling me to appreciate the language of music. In the final stages of my edits, the floor of my office in the Hutchins Center at Harvard University was an unwitting collaborator in enabling my habit of scattering printed pages to edit – striped carpet, you rock.

Thanks to Franziska Rentzsch for listening to, and encouraging me, to my siblings for keeping me grounded, to Naana Orleans-Amissah and Nana Akua Anyidoho for patiently reading and commenting on early drafts of *Azúcar*, to Anita Mensah for making me smile, to Courttia Newland for setting me on this prose journey, to my wonderful French translator

Sika Fakambi for working alongside me as always, and, most of all, my late Auntie Sylvia and Uncle Bill for providing me with a home to write in. It breaks my heart that this book wasn't finished while they were still alive, but I feel it carries something of their humour and tenacity.

Hisham Matar, Ellah Wakatama, Ahmed Akasha, Essie Blankson-Turner, Hervé Bullot, Patrice & Gabrielle Châteauneuf, Ivan Nartey, Magdalene Abraha, Mark Freeman, Ben Okri, Alexandra Kudolo, Jacob Sam-La Rose, Bema Frimpong, Niall O'Sullivan, Ebow Essilfie, Suzanne Alleyne, Nicola Griffiths, Casey Abaraonye, Meron Dagnew, Dean Ricketts, Prishani Satyapal, Kobina Graham, Diana Matar, Roger Robinson, Warsan Shire and Kwesi DeGraft-Johnson, without your friendship and quiet support, the world would be a very dull place to grow old in.

In 2013, I was having breakfast with the great Ngugi wa Thiong'o when he told me that he found it healthy to stay jealous of younger writers; he called it productivity jealousy, and I have adopted the practice. I would like to thank Laila Lalami, Courttia Newland, Kamila Shamsie, Jose Eduardo Agualusa, Leone Ross and Maaza Mengiste for making me jealous and keeping me working.

Finally, thanks to my incredible children, Naa Naa, Fifi and Afi, for showing me every day that imaginations grow and hopes bloom and that love is a vast, many-tentacled thing. And to my mother for 'writing' me. And to my father who planted music in me: your dream lives, Pops.

ABOUT THE AUTHOR

Nii Ayikwei Parkes is a Ghanaian-British writer and editor who has won acclaim as a children's author, poet, broadcaster and novelist. Winner of multiple international awards including the ACRAG award, his novel *Tail of the Blue Bird* won France's two major prizes for translated fiction – Prix Baudelaire and Prix Laure Bataillon – in 2014, and was praised by the *Financial Times* as "a beautifully written fable... simple in form, but grappling with urgent issues." Nii Ayikwei is the founder and senior editor at flipped eye publishing, a leading small press, and serves on the boards of *World Literature Today* and the AKO Caine Prize, and was chair of judges for the 2020 Commonwealth Prize. He is the author of two collections of poetry *The Makings of You* (2010) and *The Geez* (2020), both published by Peepal Tree Press. Before these were the poetry chapbooks: *eyes of a boy, lips of a man* (1999), *M is for Madrigal* (2004), a selection of seven jazz poems, and *Ballast* (2009), an imagination of the slave trade by balloon. His poem, "Tin Roof" was selected for the Poems on the Underground initiative in 2007, and in the same year he was awarded Ghana's National ACRAG award for poetry and literary advocacy. He has held visiting positions at the University of Southampton and California State University, Los Angeles, and is currently a Hutchins Fellow at Harvard University.

The Makings of You
ISBN: 9781845231590; pp. 80; pub. 2010; £8.99

Nii Ayikwei Parkes' début collection encompasses the story of
a triangular trade in reverse – a family history that goes from
the Caribbean back to Sierra Leone, and in his own life from
London to Ghana, and back again.

His gift as a poet is for the most rewarding kind of storytelling, including those stories told with wit and an engaging
ambivalence about himself. His narratives move unerringly to
a perfect punch-line, but in the collection as a whole there is
a refreshing lack of complacency in his willingness to move
out of his comfort zone and explore areas of imaginative
fantasy, as in his "Ballast" series, a tour de force of
defamiliarisation, where he imagines how the slave trade
would have gone had its mode of transport been the hot air
balloon, rather than the slave ship.

There is much humour, but it comes from a family tradi-
tion of knowing that "our jokes weren't really funny, they
were just sad/ stories we learned to laugh at". Like all poets
with a largeness of heart, with no embarrassment about
embracing the deepest feelings, Parkes has an especial sensi-
tivity to the promise and acute sensitivities of childhood, both
his own and others'.

Nii Ayikwei Parkes's poem "Barter" from *The Makings of You*
was featured on tube train posters throughout London as part
of the fantastic "Poems on the Underground", celebrating 150
Years of the London Underground.

The Geez
ISBN: 9781845234775; pp. 72; pub. 2020; £9.99

Concerned with the phase of life sometimes referred to as the midlife crisis, *The Geez* navigates the blurred lines between age and youth; the real and the imagined; what is seen and what is – what catches the gaze and what lies beneath. Through four sections, the collection moves from play, to love, to gossip and to explorations of the intersections of self and contemporary culture, including poems inspired by blues legends, riffing on the myth of the crossroads, as well as a love letter to the African diaspora.

"*The Geez* is a core-shifting collection. Each section is an electric shock to the senses. Nii is writer of precision, of ritualistic delicacy, his words are a symphony and every note in this masterpiece is a masterpiece in itself. How lucky is the reader to be taken on a journey through the self, where they are shown the real in the imagined and the imagined in the real. Each poem is a shovelling through the soil of one's perception, the richness, the grit, the depth. This brilliant collection is the sum of breathing, of loving, loathing, thinking, believing, grieving, thirsting, reaching and reaching." — Caleb Femi

"The questing and questioning poems of Nii Ayikwei Parkes' *The Geez* range across time and continents, synthesising the broad and resistant histories of the global black community, with intimate questions about love, family, parenthood and grief. Formally inventive, the collection sings with its own music and with a consciousness of the transformative power of black music in the diaspora. It is rare to find a book so fiercely political and emotionally intimate. A compelling and captivating collection." — Hannah Lowe

"A beautiful, beautiful book." — Khaled Mattawa